Dear Reader,

One of the worst things about being a creative person is imagining worrisome what-ifs: What if I left the bathroom fan running before I left home for the day? Would it short out and set the house on fire? What if I wrote a sensitive e-mail to a friend and accidentally copied everyone in my address book? Or what if the salesperson who processed my transaction used my personal information to charge purchases to my credit card? Worse, what if I couldn't prove that I didn't make those purchases?

Fortunately, none of those things have happened to me, but in *Words of Wisdom*, Mary is the victim of credit card fraud. What makes her problem even more disconcerting is that she's a stickler about finances and always takes care with her personal information. If it can happen to her, it can happen to anybody.

In addition to her money problems, Mary must consider the possibility of dating again. Since I'm a romantic at heart and have published a number of romance novels, I found it a lot of fun to plop her back into the dating scene, despite her protests, and watch how that turned out.

Best of all, while writing about Mary's involvement with expectant mothers-to-be, I learned the happy news that my daughter is expecting her first child. By the time this book sees print, a precious baby girl will be brightening our lives. Your prayers for a healthy and happy life for our little one would be greatly appreciated.

Love and grace,
Carolyn Greene

Secrets of Mary's Bookshop

A New Chapter
Rewriting History
Reading the Clues
The Writing on the Wall
By Word of Mouth
A Book by Its Cover
Poetry in Motion
Missing Pages
Between the Lines
By the Book
Disappearing Acts
A Classic Case
Cover Story
A Thousand Words
The Lost Noel
Work in Progress

SECRETS *of* MARY'S
BOOKSHOP

Words of Wisdom

Carolyn Greene

Guideposts

New York

Acknowledgments

Every attempt has been made to credit the sources of copyrighted material used in this book. If any such acknowledgment has been inadvertently omitted or miscredited, receipt of such information would be appreciated.

"From the Guideposts Archives" originally appeared in *Daily Guideposts 2008*. Copyright © 2007 by Guideposts. All rights reserved.

Cover and interior design by Müllerhaus
Cover illustration by Ross Jones, represented by Deborah Wolfe, Ltd.
Typeset by Aptara, Inc.

Printed and bound in the United States of America
10 9 8 7 6 5 4 3 2 1

To Stephanie and Chad,

If God had lined up all the children in the world and
allowed me to choose any two,
I still would have picked you.

ACKNOWLEDGMENTS

Many thanks to Andy Crenshaw, former credit card fraud investigator, for taking the time to play "what if" with me in the plotting of this book. And to Helen Beka at the Copley Place Mall in Boston for describing the area to me. If there are mistakes in either matter, they are solely mine.

Words of Wisdom

ONE

·◆◆·

The twenty-five-degree Cape Cod temperature wouldn't be so bad if it weren't for the capricious January wind that danced around Mary Fisher's wool coat. She tucked the thick scarf closer around her neck and bustled from the parking lot into the "pay as you may" health clinic.

Inside, the receptionist looked up from her work and presented her with a wide smile. A headset rested on her thick black, spiral-curled hair, and her kind eyes—set wide against smooth brown skin—gave her an appearance of warmth and sweet innocence. The desk, as tidy as its occupant, sported all the usual office trappings—stapler, letter opener, hole punch—and each one was labeled with the owner's name.

"You must be Jada," Mary said after reading the labels.

The young woman's eyes widened even more. "How did you know?"

Mary laughed and swept a hand toward the desk. The only thing not labeled was the receptionist.

"Oh, these." Jada shrugged. "My stuff has a tendency to walk away." Her tone implied she had gone beyond being annoyed by the situation and now merely accepted it as inevitable.

Mary pulled the completed application out of her purse and started to introduce herself.

"I know who you are," Jada interrupted. "You're the lady who owns Mary's Mystery Bookshop over on Main Street."

"You're a reader?" Since she'd opened the shop after moving to Ivy Bay after her husband's passing a couple of years ago, Mary had come to know some of Ivy Bay's most avid readers, but this young woman didn't look familiar.

"*Um*, no. Not enough time, unfortunately. Our nurse-practitioner mentioned you were coming."

Mary thought about how many people in their late teens and early twenties had fallen away from reading, and alternated between isolating themselves with their electronic gadgets and trying to fit in with their peers.

"Phlebotomy classes and some extra duties at work are taking up all my time right now," Jada said, blowing her theory to bits. "Here, let me take that. Katina said you'd be dropping off an application to volunteer."

Jada pulled the application out of the envelope, looked it over, and placed it faceup on the counter that bordered her desk.

"It's really sweet of you to lead a book discussion group for our young pregnant clients. We've seen an unusually high number of teens lately, and I'm sure they could use the perspective of someone who's a little older and wiser."

The timing had been perfect, actually. Mary had received a call from her son about her granddaughter Daisy, who seemed to be trying too hard to fit in with her friends. Unfortunately, one of those friends was overeager to gain the acceptance of her boyfriend, and Mary and her son worried that Daisy might get the idea that it was acceptable to make similar unwise choices for herself.

Well, Daisy lived in Chicago—too far away for Mary to take under her wing in person and reinforce the values her parents were trying to instill—but perhaps Mary could reach out to some local girls who'd already made questionable choices and who could use a mentor at a pivotal time in their lives. When her sister Betty had become involved in the Winter Carnival fund-raising effort for the clinic and learned of the many young women in need, she had suggested a book club group geared specifically toward their interests.

"I have to go to the back to do some filing," Jada said, "but I'll let Katina know you're here."

Mary took a seat in the waiting area, next to an older woman who confided that she was there to be immunized so she could accompany a group from her church on a ten-day mission trip. On the nearby sofa, a fit-looking teenage boy sat with his mother, holding a medical form. Probably a baseball player getting a physical exam prior to the start of the season. And, in a chair, all alone, a shy young woman— possibly still in her teens—toyed with her fingernails. Her head was bent and shoulders hunched forward as if she were trying to be invisible. Not likely, given that she must be at least six months pregnant.

"There you are!" The waiting area exploded in sound and activity as a fortyish woman in nurse's scrubs burst into the room and gestured for Mary to join her at the reception desk. Like the girl who sat across from Mary, the nurse appeared to be pregnant also, perhaps three or four months away from delivery. "I'm Katina Stanley, the nurse-practitioner. Let's get you signed on the dotted line, and after your background check clears in about a week or so, you'll be good to go."

Mary looked over the forms, and Katina idly rubbed her belly. The nurse laughed, the sound a little too loud for the small room.

"This baby is my fourth," the expectant mom announced. "A little 'PS' nine years after the last one. The first kid is getting ready to head off to college, so I'm hoping this one will earn its own scholarships. I don't have a clue how to pay four tuitions otherwise. It's like there's something in the water in Ivy Bay," Katina said, referring to the old wives' tale that always popped up whenever two or more expectant moms were seen together in one place. "You can't swing a cat around here without hitting someone who's preggers." She glanced over at the boy sitting with his mother. "Present company excluded, of course."

When Betty had filled Mary in on the needs of the clinic, she had mentioned the stellar reputation of this nurse-practitioner. The clinic in general, and Katina in particular, drew not only low-income patients, but also quite a few who could well afford to pay. Mary supposed Katina's boisterous personality indicated a high energy that she tapped into to give each patient her full attention.

"Congratulations on your new addition," Mary said, while hunting through her purse for a pen.

"Here, I'll get you one." Katina stepped behind the desk and moved the tidy piles of paper in her search for a pen. When none turned up, Mary wondered if Jada had neglected to label her pens and they had "walked away," or if she had hidden them from desk marauders such as this.

Having turned up empty-handed, Katina opened drawers until she found a denim purse.

"Please don't bother," Mary told her. "I'm sure there's a pen in my car. It'll only take a minute."

"No need to go all the way out there," Katina insisted. "Jada's always hiding her pens. There's bound to be one in here. She won't mind." At that, Katina plunged her hand into the purse and pulled out a slender flashlight, pink lip gloss, a plastic spoon, and finally two pens. She handed one of the pens to Mary and put the rest of the stuff back. "Here you go. Sign away."

Mary turned the pen over in her hand and read the name on the label wrapped around its barrel: *Jada*. A wave of undeserved guilt swept over her for using the purloined pen, and she found herself hurrying through her signature to avoid being caught with it.

Katina took the background waiver from her and laid it faceup on Jada's desk, then stuck another form in front of her. "I saw on your application that you're widowed. While you're practicing your John Hancock, why not go ahead and register for the Cupid Couples matchup? The couples will be announced Valentine's weekend at the Winter Carnival. Then you go out on at least one date with the person and see if lightning strikes. All proceeds benefit the clinic."

That last bit ordinarily would have been enough for her to dig deep into her wallet to help, but it hadn't been so terribly long since she'd lost John, her husband of just over forty years. Quite honestly, she didn't think anyone else would ever measure up to the love of her life.

"No, I'll leave that for the younger people." People who didn't have memories of a deceased spouse whom they held as a standard against which all other men were judged. "I'll be happy to donate the twenty-dollar entry fee, but I'm not interested in meeting anyone at this time."

"But we need more entries in your age bracket." Katina moved closer and brazenly stuffed the form into Mary's handbag. "Take it home with you, think about it, and return it to me when you show up for your first book club session with the girls."

Mary wasn't going to change her mind, but rather than argue the point, she closed the flap on her purse and tucked it under her arm to keep the nurse from adding anything else.

"Seriously," Katina said, her tone softening from her earlier booming introduction, "thank you for volunteering with the girls. I'd love to mother all of them myself, but there's only enough time to be their nurse during the brief appointments." She nodded toward the girl in the waiting area. "Brianna has said she's interested in joining your book club, and when I mentioned it to another patient, Chelsea, a few minutes ago, she said she'd come too."

Katina held out her hand, and Mary shook it, noting the dry, sandpapery skin that often accompanied the job of nursing. Katina's take-charge attitude dissolved, and her gray eyes expressed a sincerity that changed her features from ordinary to pretty.

"These girls need someone like you," the nurse added. "Someone who can share a few words of wisdom at a pivotal time in their lives. Knowledge they can perhaps pass along to their children."

A twinge of guilt stabbed at Mary for having found the woman's initial impression somewhat abrasive. After all, it took a real go-getter to accomplish all that Katina did for the clinic's patients while trying to find time for her own growing family. Her heart seemed to be in the right place.

As for Mary's heart, its place was still with her darling John. She would pass the Cupid Couples flyer to someone else. Someone who was ready for the possibility of meeting and falling in love with someone new.

———

At home, Mary found her sister bustling around the living room, getting the house they shared ready for an upcoming meeting of the Winter Carnival planning team. Perhaps *bustling* was an overstatement. Even on the best of days, Betty moved carefully to avoid causing pain to joints that had been ravaged by rheumatoid arthritis. Today seemed to be one of her more energetic days, for which Mary was grateful. Two years older than her own sixty-two years, Betty had an enthusiasm for whatever project she poured herself into that easily matched that of any thirty-year-old. Her body, unfortunately, couldn't always keep up with her zeal.

Pushing aside lingering thoughts of Cupid Couples and her car troubles, Mary set the cat carrier down on the floor and opened the front flap. As usual, Gus, her blue-eyed, gray bit of fluff, had spent the day with her at the bookshop, alternately entertaining customers or ignoring them. He paused at the opening, blinked as if assessing whether he truly wanted to come out, then eased himself through the door as if he were doing Mary and Betty a favor by blessing them with his presence.

Betty paused in her task of straightening sofa pillows. "What's the matter?"

Despite her own pains, her sister was always more concerned about what bothered others. Mary put the cat carrier away and tidied Betty's collection of gardening and interior-decorating magazines before answering. "Valentine's Day is coming up," she said at last.

A widow herself, Betty must have understood exactly what Mary meant. For most singles, it was a time of excitement and possibilities, but for them, the day served as a reminder of all they had once had, and all they'd lost.

"Worse, Katina Stanley practically twisted my arm to register for the Cupid Couples matchup. I offered to donate the fee without entering, but she insists she needs more people to pair up in my age bracket."

Betty sat on the sofa and placed the fluffed pillow behind her back. Her gaze held both sympathy and understanding. Good, she would confirm that Mary was doing the right thing. Take her off the uncomfortable hook Katina had tried to snare her with.

"You should do it," Betty said.

Gus jumped onto the sofa and plopped himself down beside Betty, his back perfectly positioned under her hand for a convenient massage. Betty obliged him, stroking her bent fingers through his gray fur while Mary picked her jaw up off the floor.

"I thought you would be on *my* side," Mary protested.

"I am, which is why I think you should give it a try." While Mary searched for words to argue her point, Betty quietly added, "It's just one date. It's not like you have to marry the guy. And who knows, maybe you'll even surprise yourself by having a good time."

It wasn't the response Mary had expected—or wanted—to hear. Her instinct was to argue with Betty and explain why going on a date was a bad idea, but her sister wouldn't have offered such a suggestion lightly.

"I'll give it some thought," she said grudgingly. "Maybe I should do it."

Her sister grinned, apparently having noticed her noncommittal response and smoothly changed the subject. "Earlier today, I noticed a package on the front porch. But when I went out to bring it in a little while later, it wasn't there."

"That's odd. Are you sure you saw a package? There's a tan cat in the neighborhood that's been peeking in the window at Gus lately. Maybe you mistook him for a cardboard box."

Betty tilted her head and pulled a long-suffering expression. "I may wear reading glasses on occasion, but I can tell the difference between a cat and a box."

Mary grinned. "Maybe the cat knocked the package off the porch. I'll go take a look."

She returned a moment later. She hadn't ordered anything to be delivered, and to her knowledge, Betty wasn't expecting any packages either. And neither of them had a birthday or other special occasion coming up.

"Perhaps the new postal carrier delivered it to the wrong place. And when he figured out his mistake, he came back for it."

Betty pursed her lips as if considering the possibility. "Rosalba wouldn't have made that kind of mistake. Or Bob Hiller either. The post office should have had Bob pick up our route, like he usually does, when she went on maternity leave."

Most of the time, Bob delivered the mail to their neighborhood, but lately Rosalba had been filling in on part of his route so he could help the postmistress with some special projects at the post office.

"Rosalba or Bob will be back soon enough. We need to be patient with the temporary guy while he learns the ropes." Since Mary was usually at work when the mail was delivered, she hadn't encountered the new carrier yet, but Betty had told her about his surly attitude. "And if a package had been meant for one of us, we'll find out soon enough when someone calls to ask if we received it."

"Too bad there wasn't a new car in that package. Yours sounded pretty bad when you pulled into the drive," Betty said, moving on to the other subject that had been bothering Mary. "Maybe it's time to replace it."

Despite the truth in her sister's words, she couldn't bring herself to part with it. John had helped her pick out the silver Impala and had taken care of the maintenance on it as a love-gift to her. The car had transported the two of them here for vacations and family visits, and the memories of their travels together seemed embedded in the very fabric of the vehicle.

After John had passed on and she returned to Ivy Bay to live with Betty, the car's maintenance had been taken over by Honest Wayne's, a local dealership and repair shop.

"I'm worried about your safety," Betty insisted.

Mary nodded, appreciating her sister's concern. She had taken a look at some of the cars on the lot a couple of weeks ago, and her application for a loan had been approved. Unfortunately, none of the cars available at the time had appealed to her. "I still haven't made up my mind what I want to do. Wayne said he'll keep an eye out for a newer Impala, if that's what I want. But, honestly, it wouldn't be the same."

"Well, at least let me give you a ride to your prayer group tomorrow." The scent of Betty's mouthwatering meat loaf wafted to them from the kitchen, and Betty seemed to take that as a cue to get up and check on it as she strategized Mary's transportation. "From there, you can walk to work or get a ride from one of the prayer groupies. Then after my Winter Carnival meeting, I'll pick you up at the bookshop, and we can take your car in for repairs. Even if you decide to sell it, it'll go faster if the transmission is in good working order."

Mary followed her into the kitchen. "Thanks. I'll take you up on the rides tomorrow, but I have to wait on spending any money on the car until I refinance the mortgage on the bookshop."

Real estate interest rates had recently dropped significantly. As a responsible steward of her money, Mary knew that getting a better deal was the right thing to do. The refinancing would cover the extra expense for the car and the books she needed to order for the upcoming Main Street sidewalk sale in the spring, as well as lower her monthly mortgage payments and save money in the long term. Ordering the books in addition to her usual bookstore inventory would hit her hard in the pocketbook at first. However, because the sale was scheduled to be held between two major historical reenactments—and those reenactors were known to be avid purchasers of historical mysteries–she fully expected to see a tidy profit from the investment.

"I could float you a loan." Betty opened the oven door, and Mary grabbed pot holders to pull out the meat loaf.

Although Betty called it a loan, Mary knew it would be a gift. Her sister could well afford it, having married into a well-to-do family and being a good financial steward in her own right. Even so, Mary couldn't ask her sister to support her bookstore.

"Thank you," she said, grateful for Betty's love and generosity. "It shouldn't take long to get the shop refinanced, and my temporary cash-flow crunch should ease up at that time. But in the meantime, I'd appreciate a ride to work or the loan of your car."

"By all means."

No matter what Mary had asked for, no matter how big her request, she knew Betty would have answered with the same easy "yes." With a heart like that, it had made her own decision to move in and help Betty during her time of delicate health an easy one.

They sat down to the table, which practically overflowed with delicious home-cooked food, and Mary gave thanks for all they shared. She was already so blessed, and it made her feel a tiny bit guilty to ask God for more, to ask for a quick and uncomplicated loan approval.

"*Eww*, that's whack!" said sixteen-year-old Kaitlyn. "Why would anybody do that?"

The youngest of the moms-to-be, Kaitlyn was the most exuberant in her comments and in her reactions to whatever topic they discussed. Mary loved her complete engagement in their discussions and hoped the teen was this involved in her schoolwork.

Kaitlyn's wide mouth pulled into a grimace of revulsion, and her eyes almost disappeared into brown crescents. Despite her comical reaction and light makeup—a touch of mascara—she looked very pretty. An athletic girl with skin still slightly golden from playing last fall's sports, Kaitlyn flipped her taffy-colored curls over her shoulder in a dramatic move, as if hiding behind her curtain of hair would shield her from the Bible story Mary just read aloud to them.

Mary grinned as all four of the girls automatically put their hands to their bellies in a protective gesture. All ranged from four to nearly eight months along in their pregnancies, and all were under the age of twenty. Now a week into February, the group already had a couple of book discussion sessions behind them and the members had started to build a rapport with one another.

Mary had quickly come to care for all of them, Brianna Bellamy, Chelsea Lambert, and Kaitlyn Moore in particular, perhaps because they were the unwed mothers, and Mary's heart went out to them in their circumstances. Nineteen-year-old Tamera Hodges, a cute, petite blonde, was the only married one in the group. And she sometimes used her seniority in age and marital status to position herself as second in charge of the group, after Mary.

After learning that the Bible was Mary's favorite book of all time, the girls had asked her to open their meetings with devotional readings and close each session with a prayer and a few words of wisdom about parenting. Now she was beginning to second-guess her decision to read the story of Solomon and the two mothers from the third chapter of First Kings.

"I think you've got it wrong," Chelsea said before Mary had a chance to respond. "The point of Solomon's decision isn't to show him as a jerk of a king, but to show a mother's bond with her baby."

A brunette with a heart-shaped face, blue eyes, and porcelain skin, Chelsea looked like an expensive china doll. As the daughter of corporate executives, she had learned an elegant composure at an early age and always seemed to know just what to say and how to say it. Mary especially liked how she could disagree with the others without coming across as disagreeable.

Brianna tentatively raised her hand. "Isn't it saying we're not supposed to wish we had somebody else's kid? That we're supposed to be happy with the one God gave us?"

It had taken a lot for the shy, sandy-blonde girl to speak up. For some reason, Brianna seemed to think that because she came from a poor family, her opinion was somehow less valuable than the others'. Interestingly, her modest background seemed not to matter to Chelsea, and the two girls had quickly become tight friends.

Mary wanted to acknowledge Brianna's courage in speaking up. "That's a good point. There will be some trying times, and you may imagine other people's children are easier to deal with than your own. It's good to remember that God matches us with the circumstances and people in our lives for a reason."

Chelsea reflected on that for a moment and added another observation. "Maybe the story is also about how mothers are willing to sacrifice to protect their kids."

Yes, this Bible story had been the right choice, after all. It had gotten them thinking. One of the girls was nineteen and married, the rest unmarried. Their family backgrounds ranged from wealthy to poor, close-knit to troubled, and high school graduates to current student. Each of the girls was as unique as her take on the story of Solomon and the two mothers. Mary silently asked God to help them take away the message they were meant to receive from the verses.

"Let's talk about *The Midwife Mystery*," Tamera suggested. "I want to know why she made the husband go boil water. Was that the old-time way of killing germs, or was she just trying to get him out of the room?"

The girls had chosen the book from a handful Mary had suggested and offered a number of insightful comments. She answered a couple of general questions about how childbirth experiences had changed from the time of this historical novel to today, but quickly changed the subject back to the plot of the story. Although she'd had some nursing training several decades ago, she didn't feel qualified to discuss the medical aspects of bringing a child into the world. Besides, the quirky characters in the story gave the group members plenty of other things to talk about.

Much too soon, Mary had to wrap up their conversation. A collective groan echoed through the room, prompting her to explain the need to finish on time. "My granddaughter is here, visiting from Chicago, and my sister will be showing up to give me a ride home very soon."

Kaitlyn looked concerned. "Why don't you drive? Did you have your license taken away?" The girl went on to volunteer that her brother's license had been revoked after being caught with an open container in his car.

Mary's heart bled for the girl and her brother. She wished she could fix the troubles of all the girls in this room, but that was unrealistic, and even trained professionals couldn't claim such results. The best she could do was be their friend, listen, care, and perhaps offer a balanced perspective seasoned with six decades of life experience.

"I drive," she said. "My car needs a new transmission, so until it's repaired, my sister is giving me rides."

Chelsea nodded. "I'm staying with my grandmother, who lives fairly close to you. My boyfriend is going to pick me up, but I'm sure he wouldn't mind giving you a ride."

Chelsea's parents lived in a well-to-do area of Quincy, about an hour's drive away, and the girl had spent most of her summers in Ivy Bay with her grandmother, which was how she had met her boyfriend.

"Thank you, but I'm sure Betty is already on her way." If Mary were going back to the bookshop, it would be a bit of a walk, but the commute from the clinic to their house required a car, or at least a bike during warmer weather, to get there. Still, she appreciated the offer.

Before the closing prayer, they all settled on the next meeting date and time and chose their next piece for discussion. For convenience, they had agreed to alternate reviewing a novel one week with a short piece the next. In addition to varying the lengths of their reading, the girls found it easier to adjust the meeting times from session to session rather than try to stick to hard-and-fast dates and times.

"If our schedules are this busy now," Brianna said after a bit of negotiating to find a common date that suited them all, "imagine what they'll be like after our babies come."

Mary grinned. Having experienced her own two children and three grandchildren, she knew firsthand how little ones can wreck even the most carefully planned schedules.

"I suggest you get your rest now, while you can."

After the girls left, Mary returned the health clinic's meeting room back to order and peeked out the window into the parking lot to check for Betty's car. No sign of it yet.

She picked up her purse, waved good-bye to Jada, and headed to the front of the building so Betty wouldn't have to come looking for her. She waited inside the glassed front door where it was warm, and smiled as she thought of the sincere discussions that had been sparked by the mystery novel. Each girl had brought her own unique perspective to the topic, and they had all learned something as a result, including Mary.

The cell phone rang in her purse, and she checked the number. The mortgage company.

She clicked the Connect button, hopeful that the refinancing loan had finally been approved so she could move forward with fixing the car and ordering books for the spring sidewalk sale. She'd been assured they would have an answer by the end of the week. Now that it was Friday afternoon, this must be her answer.

It wasn't the loan officer, but the secretary who called.

Mary tried not to read too much into the fact that the loan officer hadn't placed the call herself. Maybe it was such a straightforward approval, all it needed was a rubber stamp.

"I'm calling for Mrs. Hamblen because she wasn't feeling well today and had to leave the office early," the caller said.

"Oh, I'm sorry to hear that." Mary made a mental note to add the bank official to her ever-growing prayer list.

"Unfortunately, I have some slightly bad news," she said.

Mary groaned. "Another delay?"

The woman hesitated. "Not exactly."

The secretary paused again, as if searching for the words to break the news to her gently. The problem was that the hesitation gave Mary's imagination an opportunity to scroll through a variety of worst-case scenarios.

"Your refinancing approval has been put on hold due to a high balance on your credit card."

TWO

◆◆◆

"My credit card?" How could there be a high balance on Mary's credit card when she seldom used it? And on the rare occasions when she did charge a purchase, she nearly always paid off the balance the following month. "I don't understand. I'm very careful with my credit. And I try never to carry a balance."

"It's not so much the balance itself," the woman explained. "What kicked it out was the fact that the card was recently opened and the account has already had frequent activity."

"There must be some mistake," she persisted. "It's been years since I opened a credit account."

"Really? It's a local business. Maybe you agreed to open a card during a transaction and then forgot about it. Cashiers are always offering me gifts and discounts to open new charge cards."

"I don't think I'd forget about it if I were using it enough to jeopardize my refinancing."

"Oh yeah. Right."

"What's the name of the bank that issued the card?"

The secretary hesitated, as if considering how much to tell her, and finally said, "I'm not authorized to give that information." Then, in a quiet voice, "I've probably already said too much."

Mary reached up and tugged her hair, a nervous gesture that did nothing to help the situation but gave her an outlet for the helpless frustration that threatened to bubble over into words she'd be unable to take back.

"Can you at least tell me if the information on the new credit account matches my information *exactly*? Name, address, Social Security number? Maybe there's another Mary Fisher whose account got mixed up with mine."

"Another Mary Fisher in Ivy Bay?"

She gave a sigh of frustration. "Humor me. Maybe there's a typo. A transposed number." Something. Anything to explain away what was strongly looking like a case of identity theft.

She waited while the young woman riffled papers and whispered under her breath as she compared the data.

"Nope. Exactly the same."

Mary considered her options. She could continue to press for more information and perhaps get the young woman in trouble for asking her to breach protocol and overstep her authority. Or she could wait until Mrs. Hamblen returned tomorrow and get the information she needed to straighten out this matter.

Mary had a thousand questions, but unfortunately, the young woman who called with the news would provide no further details. Fortunately, there was a third option. "What about another loan officer? Or Mrs. Hamblen's supervisor. Surely, there's someone who can answer a few questions."

"I'm sorry, but most of our staff is at a conference this week. And the few who stayed behind are either tied up at the moment or they've gone home for the day."

Ah. So that's how a secretary had been tasked with making the call.

"Mrs. Hamblen should be back in the morning, and I'm sure she'll answer your questions at that time."

Mary thanked the woman for her help, limited as it was, and pressed the Disconnect button. A knot of worry tightened in her stomach. Sure, the loan hadn't been denied and had merely been placed on hold, but the delay would certainly impact her transportation and might possibly affect the delivery date of the books that needed to arrive in time for the sidewalk sale.

Betty's car pulled up to the front walk. Mary opened the clinic door and stepped out into the cold February afternoon.

Unfortunately, those little financial problems paled next to the issues with the overloaded credit card—a card she had neither opened nor used.

This wasn't just a simple reporting error or a random mistake. Someone right here in Ivy Bay, judging by the fact that the credit account had been opened at a local business, had stolen her identity. And it was clear that someone was intent on buying as much as possible before the credit line was cut off.

Betty waited for her to slide into the passenger seat, then met her gaze. "Bad day?"

"You could say that." Mary worked, paid her bills, gave thanks to God for the blessings, and yet some freeloader had taken it upon him- or herself to enjoy the fruits of her labor while trashing her credit rating.

In the book of Romans, God had said, "Vengeance is mine." Well, He could have all the vengeance He wanted. Until then, Mary would work on finding the perpetrator and bringing him or her to justice through the legal system.

———

That evening, Betty carried the silver tray full of hors d'oeuvres to the coffee table. The tray wobbled in her hands, threatening to spill the attractive finger food on her guests.

Mary had given her sister a brief rundown of the unpleasant news she'd received today, and she wondered if Betty's unsteady hands were caused by stress over her financial situation or by the arthritis that often presented its symptoms at the most inconvenient times. Either way, it concerned Mary that Betty had to continue fighting this physical battle. She quickly prayed that God would give her sister comfort. Then she reached for the tray, but her granddaughter beat her to it.

Daisy hastily stepped forward to take the platter. "Do let me get that for you, Auntie Bets."

Mary stared at the beautiful young girl who looked so much like Mary's son Jack—who in turn favored his father— that it almost made her cry with joy to see those special elements of her loved ones in Daisy's precious face. But this girl did not sound or look anything like the granddaughter she knew.

A designer top gathered under Daisy's small bust and cut a diagonal line across her slim waist. It seemed a little mature for her sixteen years. Not inappropriate, but just a little expensive for a teenager's taste. And the way Daisy spoke to Betty had sounded less like the bubbly girl Mary knew and more like Mrs. Howell on a rerun of *Gilligan's Island*.

"What a sweet girl," Katina said from the comfort of the blue-and-white-striped damask sofa. "And you look so pretty."

Daisy passed the tray around to the members of the Winter Carnival committee, then set it on the coffee table by the silver tea service. Betty loved to go all out when entertaining. Relieved of her burden, Betty took a seat with the others.

"Why, thank you ever so much," Daisy said with a coy dip of her head toward Katina. Then she feathered her fingers and stuck out her hand for an overly dainty handshake. "I'm Aster. Aster Fisher, Mary's granddaughter," she clarified.

Mary and Betty locked gazes with each other. Betty, clearly as baffled as she, lifted her shoulders to indicate she had no clue what had sparked the girl's affected behavior.

"Aster is short for Asteraceae, which is Latin for the common daisy," her granddaughter added.

Well, that explained why she chose Aster as her new nickname.

Katina laughed good-naturedly. "There's nothing common about you, honey. In fact, there's something very special and unique about you."

Something very phony. Mary wondered what her granddaughter was up to. As if to confirm her suspicion, Daisy pointedly refused to meet her eye.

Mary cleared her throat and addressed the group. "Daisy—er, Aster—arrived yesterday from Chicago and will be visiting with us for a few days. Her school was temporarily shut down after a water pipe burst."

Daisy's mother, Christa, had sent the girl to stay with Mary in hopes she could help the girl through a trying teenage phase. Although the burst water pipe was unfortunate, the timing couldn't have been better. After seeing Daisy's out-of-character behavior today, Mary understood what Christa had been talking about when she asked if the girl could come to Ivy Bay for a while. Daisy certainly needed a little extra attention until she worked through whatever was causing her to abandon her own cute personality and act like someone other than herself.

Betty took the opportunity to introduce Katina and Jada, as well as print-shop owner Jerry Avakian. Then, as if to acknowledge the different person Daisy had suddenly become, she continued her introductions to include the rest of the Winter Carnival committee, even though Daisy already knew them—neighbors Simon Rafferty and Sherry Walinski, Betty's sister-in-law Eleanor Emerson Blakely, and Chief of Police Benjamin McArthur.

Daisy, aka Aster, seemed not to notice the redundancy of the introductions. "Charmed!" She made a movement that was a knee dip short of being labeled a curtsy. "I wish I could stay and chat, but my American Lit term paper is calling. Ta-taaa!" She exited the room with a wave and a flourish.

The guests all watched with amusement, then turned their gazes to Mary, who shrugged. "Teenagers," she said simply, and they all nodded in agreement.

Although she herself wasn't on the committee and had plenty of other duties that needed to be taken care of—

finding out about that credit card that showed up on her credit report—Mary stayed to help Betty with her hostessing. Truthfully, she wanted to drop everything and investigate the credit card situation, but she was unsure where to start looking. And even if she knew the name of the bank that had issued the card, there was little she could do about it tomorrow with it being a Saturday. As for helping out with the Winter Carnival planning meeting this evening, she didn't mind lending a hand, especially since her sister was so generous to a good cause.

Chief McArthur leaned forward and poured himself a cup of tea. "I may be out of town the day of the event," he said, and several people in the room groaned. "But I'll give you the name and contact info for the officer who'll be overseeing crowd control that day."

He lifted the lid on the sugar bowl to find it empty.

Betty cut a glance at her sister-in-law as if mortified to be seen as a less-than-perfect hostess. "Oh, silly me. I forgot to fill the bowl with sugar cubes."

The chief stilled her efforts to rise. "Allow me."

As he pushed himself off the couch, a colorful chip fell out of his pocket and wedged itself beside a tufted pillow. He quickly scooped it back up and stuffed it into his pocket.

No one else seemed to notice, but Mary did. She stood to join him. "I'll show you where Betty hides the sugar."

She picked up the sugar bowl and followed the chief past the decorative table holding an overflowing basket of mail. In the kitchen, she opened a cupboard and pointed to the box of sugar cubes, then watched while he dumped them into Betty's porcelain dish.

He pointedly ignored her unasked question. "Not many people use sugar cubes anymore. Usually, you see that stuff in pink or blue or yellow packets. I prefer the real thing, myself."

His distraction tactic didn't deter her from trying to find out whether her friend was in trouble. "Have you taken up a new hobby?" she asked softly.

"Sugar connoisseur? No, but I was thinking of taking up sugar-cube sculpting in my spare time." He grinned, the simple gesture changing his expression from his usual serious demeanor to a more relaxed, approachable, and even handsome visage.

Mary waited while he joked about the weight he would gain from eating more of the cubes than he sculpted. She didn't want to make assumptions, but it concerned her that he was evading her question.

The sugar dish now full, he returned the box to the cabinet and turned back to face her. He met her gaze, his expression now as serious as hers. "It's not what you think."

He had read her mind. "And what am I thinking?"

"That you won't rest until you find out why I'm carrying a poker chip in my pocket."

"That's very astute of you." She waited another moment, hesitant to back him into a corner, but also unwilling to let the matter drop. Silence hung between them for a moment while she reached for the platter of heart-shaped chocolates Betty had made and apparently forgotten to set out for the guests.

His reluctance almost palpable, he finally looked over his shoulder as if to check for eavesdroppers, then turned back to Mary. He lowered his voice. "The department is currently working in tandem with Boston police to uncover an illicit gambling ring in the city." Then, as if embarrassed, he added, "The chip is a reminder of sorts. It keeps me focused."

Relieved, Mary let out the breath she didn't realize she'd been holding. She had never known him to gamble, and she believed he was telling the truth.

But he needn't be embarrassed to admit he held on to the chip as a tactile reminder of his mission. Some of the sleuths in the mystery novels Mary loved to read did the very same thing. Perhaps, as Chief McArthur indicated, the object prompted him to stay alert to clues. Or, as with fictional detectives, it may have reminded him of the importance of staying vigilant, a prompt to keep the deeper purpose of the investigation at the front of his mind.

"Since the investigation is still ongoing, I'd appreciate it if you wouldn't mention this to anyone," he said.

"Have you ever known me to betray a confidence?"

He grinned in acknowledgment. "Why do you think I told you?"

Mary smiled in response to the high compliment he had just paid her. Although her curiosity occasionally led her to check out local situations that sometimes involved the law, she was always respectful of his boundaries as a law enforcer. And in return, he respected her knowledge and opinions enough that he sometimes solicited her thoughts on unfolding minor crimes. She appreciated that he accepted her viewpoint when others on the force might have merely brushed her off.

"Your secret is safe with me," she said, and turned to take the chocolates out to their guests. If she dallied any longer, they might not get eaten. Then it would be up to her and Betty to finish them off. "Just promise me you'll take care."

He opened the kitchen door and held it for her. "Don't you worry about me. I'll be fine."

"It's not you I worry about. It's the criminals you're trying to apprehend that make me nervous."

Mary stepped through the kitchen door and almost collided with Katina. The plate of chocolates wobbled in Mary's hands, and the nurse jumped at the unexpected commotion.

A couple of pieces of mail fluttered from Katina's fingers and fell to the floor. Despite her cumbersome size, their guest quickly bent to pick up the papers, then placed them back in the basket.

Mary could only stand there and stare at the nurse's audacity to be going through her mail. But, considering how Katina had considered it her right to search Jada's purse for a pen, it shouldn't have surprised her.

"Oops, sorry. I didn't know you would come bursting out like that. You nearly scared the life out of me."

How was it that the person perusing her mail could manage to turn the situation around and make her feel bad for startling her? Mary's fingers automatically tightened over the plate of chocolates. "Were you looking for something?"

Katina smiled. "The bathroom. You know how it is at this stage of the game," she said, and laid a hand on her round belly. "But as I was walking past the table, I happened to notice this beautiful decorating magazine that has a special feature on outfitting a nursery. Pretty cool, huh? My kid would be the talk of the neighborhood in that room."

The brunette flipped the magazine open and displayed a peach-and-green color scheme that showcased a white crib, green overstuffed chair, and whimsical striped curtains.

If Mary had given the photo spread her full attention, she might have agreed that it was indeed a striking image. But her gaze was drawn to the other piece of mail Katina had dropped after she'd been caught by surprise—an envelope Mary had opened and set aside to handle later. Although it was nothing she would have considered classified information, the contents did contain personal data that she wouldn't want falling into the wrong hands.

Chief McArthur stepped around her, wordlessly took the plate of candies from her hand, and delivered both the chocolates and sugar cubes to the guests who were busily wrapping up one of the planning details for next week's Winter Carnival. She could tell by the way he had sidled past her that he knew something was going on between her and Katina and didn't want to get trapped in the middle.

She didn't blame him. Once again, Katina had disrespected boundaries, and Mary didn't like it any more than she suspected the clinic receptionist did once she found out her boss had rummaged through her personal belongings for a pen.

Oblivious to Mary's distress over having her privacy invaded, Katina rattled on. "A lot of our expectant patients want to know before the birth whether they're going to have a girl or boy. Not me. I'd rather wait until it's born and enjoy the surprise, y'know? So this color scheme is great because peach and green will work for either sex."

The woman's nosiness may have been harmless enough— that of a new mom searching for just the right decorating plan for her little bundle of joy. Even so, Mary couldn't help thinking about the background check she'd had to undergo before being cleared to volunteer at the health clinic. Had Katina's curiosity led her to look through the application? Maybe even use the information on it to open the credit card that now jeopardized the approval of her refinancing loan?

Mary picked up the mail basket and held it out for Katina to return the magazine to its rightful place. "The bathroom is that way," she said and pointed down the hall.

Uncomfortable with the disturbing direction her thoughts had taken, Mary pushed her suspicions aside. She waited for Katina to find the room and close the door behind her. Then she took the basket of mail to the kitchen and crossed to the pantry.

Mary didn't consider herself a mistrustful person, and she certainly didn't want to let a case of identity theft make her paranoid about a guest in her own home. No, she refused to become cynical over today's unfortunate turn of events. But she wouldn't be foolhardy either.

She set the basket on a shelf in the pantry, then closed the door.

THREE

Henry Woodrow opened the passenger door of his 1953 Chevy Bel Air, crossed an arm over his waist, and bowed grandly for Mary to enter. A year older than her, he'd been her friend since childhood, and she was grateful for the opportunity to reconnect with him after her return to Ivy Bay. They shared a lot of interests in common, and spending time with him had helped ease her transition back into the community. And, as always, he'd extended a helping hand whenever she needed one. This time, it was a ride to work. With her transmission so unreliable, she didn't want to take the chance of being stranded beside the road. In the summer she would have walked to work, but the cold February weather discouraged that.

"Where to, madam?"

His impersonation of a chauffeur prompted a giggle from Mary.

Dressed in a heavy cable-knit sweater and still carrying the remnants of a tan from spending time on his fishing boat last summer, he didn't exactly look the part of a fancy driver. Nor did he act the part. Whenever he spoke to anyone, he fixed his sea-green eyes on that person in a show of genuine interest. He was one of the most down-to-earth people in Ivy Bay, and Mary was happy to call him her friend.

She slid onto the seat of his treasured convertible and waited for him to get behind the wheel. "The bookshop, please. But I'd like to stop by the post office first, if you have the time."

"I always have time for you. But if you don't mind, first I need to drop off some fishing gear to be repaired."

"Sure thing," she agreed. "After all, you're the one who's doing me a favor."

Yesterday at church, when Betty had mentioned the trouble she'd been having with the car, Henry had immediately sought her out and offered rides any time she needed them and insisted she put his number on speed dial. Fortunately, his self-employed lifestyle allowed him the flexibility to set his own schedule.

They passed the Department of Motor Vehicles, and a short while later, he said, "Are you sure you don't want to stop here too?"

"Here" was Honest Wayne's Auto Sales and Repair. Despite the nippy weather, the ever-smiling owner stood outside on the lot, trying to reel in a customer by tempting him with a late-model domestic car.

"I've already been there. There were no cars that I liked as well as, or better than, my own. Wayne said he'd keep an eye out for a newer Impala, but I don't know if that's what I want either."

Henry slanted his knowing green eyes at her. "The new ones don't have the scent of his cologne."

He understood. His wife—the namesake for his boat *Misty Horizon*—had passed away, and he still wore the rugged, outdoorsy clothes Misty had bought for him. As for Mary, the actual scent of John's cologne was long gone, but what remained was the essence—the memory—of him in their car. Unable to speak, she merely dipped her head in acknowledgment.

Henry didn't pursue the subject further. He always seemed to know just what to say, or not. "So you'll put in a new transmission, and it'll be as good as a new used car." He grinned.

"I suppose." With John, this would have been a simple choice. But having to make the decision by herself left her open to self-doubt and second-guessing, which was not like her. As with other milestones since his passing, this would be conquered too. With God's help, of course. It always helped to remember that God was with her, even if John wasn't.

"Let me know when you're ready to take it in for repair, and I'll go with you."

"You don't need to do that." Mary had heard that some women had a man go with them for car repairs to prevent being taken advantage of, but she didn't think it was necessary in this case. More than that, she didn't want to become dependent on her friend's generosity. "I'll be taking it to Honest Wayne's. He's always been fair with me in the past."

He nodded in agreement. "Then let's stop here now and set up a date in case he needs to schedule a tow truck."

"The car still drives, albeit a bit noisily, so it shouldn't need a tow truck. Perhaps earplugs for the driver, to drown out the whine, would be nice." She laughed at the thought of wearing earplugs while forcing others on the road to endure the ever-increasing cacophony that heralded her car's presence. "But it wouldn't hurt to give Wayne a heads-up so he can order the parts and have them available when I'm ready to take the car in."

"Good. I'll be available until you get it fixed. You be sure to call me," he urged. "Don't be shy."

"Thank you. You'll be on my speed dial for the next week or so until my refinancing loan is approved." Speaking of which, she really needed to get the problem with the mysterious credit card cleared up *today*. The sooner, the better.

Her hand went to her neck and closed around the small blue sapphire pendant that had been a "just because" gift from John. Mindlessly, she let her fingers slide the tiny stone along its slim gold chain.

Henry looked over at her, his mouth set in a tense clench.

"What?" she said.

He pulled to a stop at the red light to circle the block and go to Honest Wayne's. While they waited for the light to turn green, he drew in a slow breath and let it out just as purposefully.

"We go back a long way," he said.

She nodded. "We do." All the way back to preschool, before her family had moved away from Ivy Bay. Since then, they'd kept the friendship going every summer and on holidays when her family had returned to visit. So when she'd moved back here to live after John died, it had been easy to resume their friendship.

"And I know you'd help me if I was in a pinch," he pressed.

"Of course I would."

"Then let me lend you the money to repair your car. Interest free, of course." He fixed those intense green eyes on her again. "You can pay me back when your loan comes through."

What a friend. A true friend, indeed. Though touched by his generosity, she knew he needed that money to complete off-season maintenance on his boat. A commercial fisherman, he delivered fresh fish to local merchants and restaurants, and sometimes offered chartered fishing trips. Like her and many others in this community, his livelihood depended upon tourist dollars. By this time of the year, after a winter with fewer tourists buying their products and services, local wallets had grown thinner.

"That's very sweet of you," she said, "and I really appreciate the offer. If the loan gets held up, it's good to know you're my backup." She wouldn't take him up on the offer, though. But it meant a lot to know he cared.

The light turned green, and he squinted into the feeble February sun.

She sent up a silent prayer of thanks for the blessing of Betty and Henry, both of whom had offered to help her through this car-troubling time. She just hoped she hadn't hurt his feelings by turning down his offer.

By the time they made it around the block and tracked back to Honest Wayne's, the potential customer had slipped off the dealer's hook, and he headed inside. Despite the lack of a hoped-for sale, Wayne's smile never wavered. In fact, it brightened further when he met Mary at the door.

"What can I do for the lovely Miss Mary?" He held the door open for her and followed her in. "Have you decided to trade in your Impala, after all?"

Henry waited beside his car, answering questions from a shopper who wanted to know if his antique Bel Air was for sale, so Mary endeavored to keep her conversation with Wayne short and sweet.

"I'm still making up my mind what to do," she admitted, but was pleased to notice that, even though she had not jumped to buy a new or new-to-her car from Wayne, his demeanor never changed. The smile stayed in place, and he waited for her to tell him what she wanted. "But I've decided it wouldn't hurt to get the car repaired, whether or not I end up keeping it."

"Excellent. A car in good working order is easier to sell than one that needs care," he said, affirming that she'd made a good choice for the time being. "Come with me and I'll write up a work order for you. As you can see by all the people in the waiting room, my manager is swamped. If I left you in there, your family would have to send a search crew to find you. It'll be quicker if I just do it myself."

"Thank you. My friend is waiting outside, so we both appreciate your expediting the process."

He took off his coat and hung it on a rack near the customer-service counter, then reached past the guy at the desk and picked up a preprinted form. Wayne led the way to his office, and his fashion sense brought to mind an image of a 1980s lounge singer. Hair carefully styled and sprayed into place. A heavy silver watch that may or may not have been silver, and polyester slacks that ended an inch above tasseled loafers. And then there was the loud orange-and-blue-plaid shirt that opened at the neck to reveal a thick, springy mat of dark-and-silver chest hair on which rested a silver neck chain. Dangling from that chain was what appeared to be a real, working compass.

She followed him into the office, where he turned to move a misplaced chair out of her way.

Apparently noticing her gaze on the intriguing necklace, Wayne blinked rapidly, several times in succession. "It's new," he said. "Got it on my last trip to Boston. The salesperson called it retro chic. I just think it's cool."

She took the chair he offered her. He seemed like a kid with a new toy that he wanted to show off, so she indulged him. "How interesting that the compass represents all the road trips that your satisfied customers take."

"Precisely!" he said, and pointed a finger at her as if she had just won a prize for giving the correct answer. "Sometimes, when you see something that's a perfect fit for your personality, you have to grab it, even if it means dusting off the ol' credit card."

Wayne pushed aside a bunch of papers and a pale blue box that the necklace must have come in. He seemed nervous, and his hands shook as he wrote her information on the repair order.

"We'll leave the date open for you to bring your car in. Just call me the day before, and we'll have the parts here waiting for you."

Mary hesitated. She really appreciated his promptness in handling her request, but unfortunately, she wouldn't be as prompt about retrieving the car after it was worked on. "I may not be able to get it out of the shop right away," she admitted. "There's a..."

She hesitated, uncomfortable with revealing her financial problems, even though they were not of her making.

" . . . a cash flow issue at the moment."

Wayne waved her concern away. "That's what credit is for. Last month when you applied for the car loan, you passed with flying colors."

That was last month, before the fraudulent account had been opened in her name and soiled her credit rating.

"So there's no problem if you want to pay it off in installments. Like layaway."

More like holding the car hostage until the ransom was delivered.

———

At the post office, Mary went inside to mail special-ordered books to die-hard summer customers who shopped her store all year long because they trusted her recommendations. The packages fell onto the counter with a clatter, but the postal employee managed to catch them before they tumbled to the floor.

"*Mmm*, you've been busy," Dalton said, a teasing glint in his eye. "Between you and Jerry, you're going to make me work overtime."

"Jerry Avakian?"

"Yeah, he just dumped the last batch of those Winter Carnival flyers on us for mass mailing. I might be able to go home Wednesday, if I'm lucky."

Although Dalton pretended to grumble about the workload, Mary knew him to be one of the busiest, most energetic people around. A fit, caramel-skinned man who claimed he stayed in shape by doing push-ups during TV commercials, he had shaved his head, saying he didn't have time in his busy life to primp.

"Good. Hard work will keep you out of trouble," she countered, returning his teasing with some of her own.

"How are you doing? Staying out of trouble, yourself?"

She laughed. It seemed everyone in town knew her propensity for getting involved in odd situations and mysterious happenings. People often joked that, as a mystery bookseller, she was a magnet for such dilemmas.

"All's well," she assured him, hoping the credit card conundrum would not turn out to be one of those problems she had a knack for stumbling onto. "Have you heard from Rosalba lately?"

Dalton put a package on the scale, weighed it, and printed out a label. "She and the baby are doing great. In fact, she brought him in here the other day. Cute little guy."

If he favored his mother, he was certain to be a looker.

"She'll be back at work in three or four weeks." He shook his head and seemed to think on that for a moment. "Seems like every time I turn around, someone else is having a baby. Must be something in the water. I keep telling my wife not to drink after them. Three is enough for us."

"If you see Rosalba again, tell her Betty and I miss her. Her smile is always such a treat when she delivers our mail."

From her first day on the job a few months ago, their mail carrier had seemed infused with positive energy. Because of her upbeat attitude, everybody liked her. And she and Bob Hiller, the carrier who delivered the mail to Mary's bookshop, had a standing agreement to pitch in and help each other if either one's route was particularly heavy on certain days. Unfortunately, Bob—another cheerful spirit— couldn't add her entire route to his own during the six weeks she was out on maternity leave.

"Be patient and you'll get those smiles back soon." Dalton's face clouded over, leading Mary to wonder if he had read something into what she said. She hadn't meant to imply anything negative about the temporary replacement, but Dalton had keyed in on what she'd left unsaid. "Has the temp been doing a good job? Has he been polite?"

What an odd question. She wondered if there had been complaints. "I wouldn't know. I haven't seen him on the route yet."

She didn't mention Betty's less-than-glowing opinion of the guy. Perhaps he was new and still figuring things out. They'd just have to be patient while he learned the job.

"That's him over there. Nathan Bayard." Dalton pointed to the back, just beyond a rack of sorting bins. "Got a late start today. He's going to be finishing up his route in the dark."

The man flinging mail into piles looked to be in his late forties or early fifties, although the frown that menaced his face may have made him look older than his true age. At first, his short brown hair led Mary to assume it had been rumpled by the wind, but on second look, it appeared to have been styled to appear artfully tousled. He wore a blue oxford shirt that looked more suited to an office than to physical work, and his actions were fast and methodical, almost angry.

His next movement was so subtle and quick she almost missed it. An envelope went from the pile to his shirt pocket in a blur, and in the next second, he was back to flinging envelopes to their designated bins. He looked up to catch her watching him.

Nathan blinked, scowled deeper until furrows creased his forehead, then positioned himself beyond the rack, out of sight of customers in the lobby.

Dalton leaned in and handed her the receipt. "He used to be a big-time advertising executive and owned his own company. But then the economy tanked and, well, it's been a lifestyle change for him and his wife. And when Mama ain't happy, ain't nobody happy."

That would explain the bad attitude Betty had noticed and the scowl he had thrown her way just now. Though her first inclination had been to dislike Nathan for his surly demeanor, Mary pushed her own feelings aside and decided to mention him in tomorrow's prayer group meeting.

FOUR

—◆◆◆—

Back from Tuesday morning's prayer group, Mary spent the rest of the morning and part of the afternoon helping Rebecca, her shop employee, set up a Valentine's display with romantic novels that had been traded in for mysteries. She smiled as she recalled a best-selling author who had held a book signing here a while back. The woman had started out writing romance novels and later made a midlife career switch to mystery writing. "In my thirties, I wanted hearts, love, and romance," the author had said with a teasing glint in her eye, "but when menopause hit, I wanted to kill something."

Mary set a paperback with a particularly attractive cover at the front of the pink-and-white draped table. "Did Mrs. Hamblen return my call while I was out?"

Rebecca slowly shook her head, as if sorry she couldn't give better news. Her assistant knew how important this loan was and had compiled a suggested list of books for the spring sidewalk sale. But that list would have to wait.

Over by the fireplace at the back of the shop, Daisy looked up from the paper she'd been working on. "This place has been dreadfully quiet all day."

Her opinion expressed, the girl went back to work.

At least Daisy was taking her schoolwork seriously, but Mary wondered if that nose-in-the-air tone would come through in her writing. She pulled the cell phone from her pocket and checked to see if a call had come through when she had muted it for prayer group earlier this morning, but the phone showed no missed calls. No call on the cell, none at work. At this point, Mary needed to start rattling cages.

"Which color does Gus like better: yellow or blue?" Seven-year-old Ashley held aloft two scraps of ribbon and waited for Mary's answer. Rebecca's daughter had been part of their employment arrangement. The blonde-haired, blue-eyed girl often came to the shop after school let out and usually pitched in to help, ringing up sales on the cash register or recommending children's books to customers. As a thank-you for her services, Mary sometimes treated her to a muffin from Sweet Susan's Bakery next door or sent her home with an armload of used books to read and return. And, of course, hugs.

Lots and lots of hugs.

The moment her focus shifted from the thought of her loan officer's silence to the charming little girl, Mary's tension dissolved like sugar in hot tea. Although there was no blood relationship between them, Ashley had come to feel like an honorary great-niece or granddaughter. Because Mary's own grandchildren lived outside of Ivy Bay, it was good to have Ashley here to add a touch of cuteness and cheer.

"I don't know," she said, wondering where the girl's line of questioning was going this time. "I suppose he likes both."

"Then we'll do eeny, meeny, miny, moe."

Mary's gaze drifted from Ashley to the gray cat that sat patiently in front of the little girl. A doll's tutu rested atop his head, and Mary surmised the ribbon would be tied under his chin to hold the pink tulle in place. Ashley moved the animal's paw between the ribbons and finished the childhood chant. "And you are not it." In addition to the ridiculous makeshift hat, Gus wore a decidedly morose expression but made no move to shake it off or leave.

Mary put a hand to her mouth to stifle the laugh that threatened to burst forth. Poor Gus looked both embarrassed and confused, which seemed to war with his desire to please his little friend.

A strange vibration from the area below her waistband startled her from the charming sight. The laugh that had been held in check now emerged as something more like a squeak.

And then it dawned on her. She reached into her pocket where the cell phone announced an incoming call. She must have forgotten to switch it to ring mode after setting it to vibrate mode for this morning's prayer meeting.

Mary stared down at the screen. The mortgage company. She pressed the Connect button and whispered to Ashley, "You should take the hat off Gus before he gets snagged on something." Then, to the caller, "Hello."

Daisy got up from her chair. "I'll make sure the little rascal does as she's told."

Despite her granddaughter's assurance, Mary had a hunch which child was the bigger rascal.

"Mrs. Hamblen?" Mary said into the phone. Finally. At last, this would put an end to the misery of waiting.

"I'm sorry," said the voice on the other end. "This is her secretary again. Mrs. Hamblen has a bad case of bronchitis and is taking a few days off. Quite a few people around here are sick with it." With that, the secretary covered the phone and coughed, the sound more like a bark than any human noise Mary had ever heard.

"I'm sorry. I hope you aren't coming down with it too."

"Don't worry. I didn't cough into the phone." The joke turned into another coughing spell.

Mary was less concerned about catching it than whether the young woman would hack up a tonsil.

The secretary finally recovered and got to the point of the call. "I'm sure you want to know about the credit card that's stalling your loan. Unfortunately, I don't have the information, and as I mentioned Friday, the people who can look it up are now either out sick or out of town at a conference for the rest of the week."

Mary drew in a deep breath to calm her anxiety and remind herself to speak with kindness and gentleness. "Someone is charging purchases to a credit card with my name on it. I can't just sit around and wait indefinitely for people to return to work. What can you do to help me get this identity-theft problem taken care of?"

"Now, we don't know for sure that the credit card is actually a result of identity theft." Her voice was slow and modulated, as if she were talking to a remedial student. "There could be an innocent explanation."

They had gone over this on Friday afternoon. There had been no doubt in either of their minds that someone was having a spending spree at Mary's expense. She couldn't pretend that all was hunky-dory when it was not. "An innocent explanation? Such as?"

Silence. And then, "*Umm...*"

"Come on. You said it yourself: The card was opened at a local business. We both know I didn't do it. That leaves only an identity thief."

"You were supposed to forget I said that."

Mary stopped herself from challenging the secretary's naive comment any further. Arguing with the messenger wasn't going to get her the information she needed.

"I'm really sorry," said the voice on the other end of the line. "It looks like all we can do is wait for Mrs. Hamblen or one of the others to come back to the office."

Mary thanked her and hung up the phone. No, waiting wasn't an option. She was going to have to come up with a suitable plan B.

———

"No, you do it like this." With a twinge of urgency in her voice, little Ashley again went over the cash register procedure with Daisy, who had taken a break from writing her term paper to help with the customers who had suddenly flooded the shop.

Mary looked up from the work she was doing to observe the girls' interaction. To Daisy's credit, she gave Ashley her full attention and showed no sign of irritation that a girl less than half her age was instructing her on how to use the cash register. Following the teen's calm lead, Ashley patiently called out the steps while Daisy punched the correct keys.

Smart and mature beyond her meager years, Ashley made it easy to forget how young she really was.

The bell over the door jangled, and Wayne the car dealer walked in with a bag full of books to trade.

With Ashley's guidance, Daisy finished ringing up the purchase, thanked the customer for her business, and turned back to stare at Ashley as if she were some newly discovered life-form. "You make straight As in school, don't you?"

Ashley hesitated a moment, then answered very sincerely. "My mom said it's not polite to brag."

For the second time that day, Mary nearly lost it. There had not been a hint of arrogance in the girl's answer. Just a desire to be polite and follow the social guidelines her mother had set out for her. Even so, the sweet and humble response tugged a smile across Mary's face.

Wayne walked over to Mary's end of the counter and set the bag down in front of her. "I'm glad you're so happy to see me," he said, returning the smile. "You might be even happier the next time we meet." He paused for effect, making sure he had her full attention before finishing his thought. "I've got a lead on an almost-new Impala. Should have it acquired, cleaned up, and on the lot ready for you to test-drive in a week or two."

Though he hadn't put the smile on her face, he was a pleasant guy. No need to burst his bubble by letting him know Ashley and Daisy were the ones who had tickled her spirit.

"That's great. Thank you for keeping an eye out for a newer car for me." Considering her back-and-forth emotions over whether to trade her vehicle in for a newer one, she thought it only fair to make it clear she was still on the fence.

"I hope you're not going to a lot of trouble on my behalf. On the chance that I decide to keep my Impala, will you have any trouble selling this car you found?"

"No problem. They're good cars. Shouldn't sit on the lot too long."

Relieved that he wouldn't be out financially if she changed her mind, she went about her business and emptied the paper grocery bag of novels he'd brought to trade.

Ashley's voice carried to her from the cash register. "Daisy, why don't you show Mrs. Winslow where the legal mysteries are, and I'll ring up the rest of the customers until you get the hang of things?"

"It's Aster."

"I know," Ashley said. "Like Asteraceae."

Mary turned back to Wayne, who seemed to be having an issue. Something stood out as odd, but she couldn't quite put a finger on what. And then she saw it. A bizarre little twitch vibrated under his left eye. And a jumpy energy jittered through his slim frame.

"Wayne, is everything all right with you?"

He blinked as if the nervous gesture would rid him of the weird dance taking place under his eye. "I've been having trouble sleeping," he admitted. "Maybe some new books would help me wind down."

Now that he mentioned it, Mary noticed the dark circles that accompanied the twitch. Poor thing. She felt bad for him and wondered if the stress of the car dealership was keeping him awake at night.

"As a matter of fact, I just shelved some new mysteries." She slid off the stool she had perched on. "Here, I'll show you."

He waved her off. "No need. I know where they are."

Concerned for whatever was going on with him, Mary watched him walk away, his gait stiff and uneven.

Daisy returned from the back and gave Wayne a curious glance as they crossed paths.

"I was thinking it would be nice to visit your cousins while you're here," Mary suggested. Her daughter lived with her husband and two children in Melrose, a little over an hour away. "Maybe we could meet in Boston and spend the day together."

"That would be *diviiiine*." Daisy drew out the word as if she were savoring the feel of it on her tongue. "Can we shop at Fergie's? I heard they just put out the new spring collection. It would be a crime to go to Boston without checking out the cute clothes at Fergie's."

Fergie's? Mary tilted her head, trying to figure out why her moderate-budget granddaughter would suggest shopping at such a high-end store. She was about to ask how she had the money to afford such an extravagance when Wayne returned and thumped a couple of books on the counter—Las Vegas-set mysteries in the Beating the Odds series.

"Boston, eh? Ayuh, I love that city. Go there whenever I get a Saturday off." He nudged Daisy with his elbow. "There's a great burger joint you ought to try. The place is a hole in the wall, but the food is wicked good."

Daisy listened politely as he gave her the name of the restaurant, then stepped behind the counter with Ashley. "It's my turn to ring up the sale," she told her young instructor.

Ashley crossed her arms over her chest. "Are you sure you can handle it?"

Mary almost snickered again, but this time, she stepped in to prevent hurt feelings. "If she can handle algebra, I'm sure she can handle a cash register."

Ashley stepped away from the register and gave Daisy a dubious look. "If you say so."

———

"Sweetie, what have you done with my granddaughter?"

"Are you talking to me?"

"Of course I'm talking to you, Daisy." There was no one else in the health clinic parking lot for the time being, which was why Mary had chosen this moment to question the girl about her recent behavior. "It's just that you don't seem like yourself lately."

Daisy stopped near the front door and pulled her jacket tighter around herself. "What *ever* do you mean?"

"That. The way you're talking. The clothes you're wearing." Mary paused and swept her gaze over the girl who vaguely resembled her granddaughter but who was clearly trying to be someone else. "And your hair. They're not you."

Daisy lifted a hand to the upswept pile of hair at the back of her head. "What's wrong with my hair? I think it's smokin' hot."

"Nothing. It just looks a little"—*pretentious? old? stuffy?*— "like you're on your way to prom."

"*All* the kids dress this way, and Morganna showed me how to put my hair up in a chignon. It's rockin', don't you think?"

"I think you'd be beautiful even if you shaved your head, wore a paper sack, and called yourself Farmer Jane."

Daisy waved her hand in an affected manner. "Oh, Grandma, you're a trip."

Mary put her arm around the girl's shoulders and squeezed. "If you ever feel the need to copy someone, Jesus is always a good one to imitate."

Daisy laughed and returned the hug. "I'd look ridiculous in a beard."

The plan had been for Daisy to cool her heels in the clinic waiting room while Mary conducted the book club meeting, but when the group members realized Mary's granddaughter had accompanied her, they insisted she join them in their book discussion.

Mary hesitated, debating whether her son and his wife would approve, especially since the discussions tended to be very honest and sometimes quite frank—a necessity for the members who needed straight talk, but which could be a little advanced for Daisy, who was not in their situation.

"*Aw*, let her join us," said Tamera, the oldest of the four. "We promise to keep it G-rated."

Daisy's parents, Jack and Christa, trusted Mary's judgment, and she wouldn't do anything to betray that trust. If the conversation became a little mature for Daisy's ears, she'd be there to redirect the discussion as needed. Besides, it might be a good idea for Daisy to hear these girls' perspectives, and the peer pressure some of them had succumbed to, which ultimately led to their current condition.

"C'mon," said Kaitlyn. "It would be nice to have someone my own age in here for a change, instead of all these old ladies." The girl swept a teasing gaze to indicate the other teens, but when her eyes met Mary's, she suddenly realized her faux pas. "Oh! I didn't mean—"

Rather than react with indignation, Mary laughed. "No offense taken," she said with a dismissive wave of her hand. "I'll go get Daisy now. But all of you have to promise to follow my cue if the conversation gets a little too spirited."

"Don't worry. I'll keep them in line," Tamera said, acting as if she were second in command.

Mary returned a moment later with Daisy in tow. Rather, *Aster*, which was how she introduced herself. Daisy sat between Mary and Kaitlyn.

While the rest of the group pulled out their reading material and chatted among themselves, the younger girl offered to share her book with Daisy, then proceeded to fill her in on how far along she was in her pregnancy. Kaitlyn leaned in and asked, "How old are you?"

Daisy seemed to contemplate whether it would be cool to reveal her age, then must have decided that was the one thing about herself it was okay to leave the same. "I'm sixteen," she said. "And a half."

"You're older than me. My birthday was last month."

Mary could almost see the gears turning while Daisy did the math.

"You'll be about my age when you have the baby."

Though her words were spoken softly, they attracted the attention of everyone in the room. Silence reigned. Mary could tell Daisy was putting herself in Kaitlyn's shoes, and she suspected those shoes pinched.

"That's gotta be hard. Who'll take care of the baby while you're at school?" Daisy seemed genuinely concerned.

Kaitlyn shrugged. "I'll probably get a job at the Black & White Diner, or maybe over at the bait shop. My aunt said she'd babysit for me, and the rest of my paycheck will go toward the baby's other expenses."

"But what about your diploma? You're going to need that."

"A GED is all I need."

"But how can you study for your GED if you're working all the time?" Her own sights set toward college, Daisy seemed genuinely distressed at the prospect that Kaitlyn's education would get sidetracked.

It was time to start the book discussion, but Mary was thankful that her granddaughter had recognized the drawbacks that came with having a baby at too young an age—drawbacks that came from following her friends' lead and blindly accepting their choices for herself. For now, Daisy reasoned that it was "cool" to talk and dress like her friends. But what if those friends decided having a physical relationship with a boy was cool? Would Daisy accept that choice as her own? Maybe this conversation would cause her to stop and think before following her friends into a too-intimate relationship with a boy. She hoped Daisy would commit this conversation to memory and reexamine it when faced with a similar temptation.

Unable to counter Daisy's logic, the young mom-to-be squirmed. Chelsea reached behind Mary's chair and gave Daisy a little nudge to indicate it was time to let the subject drop.

"Huh? Oh." Daisy turned a couple pages in the book she shared with Kaitlyn. "I love to hold babies. My neighbors let me babysit for them sometimes," she said, her words more of a babble than a statement. "I can't wait to meet the right guy and have kids of my own someday."

Mary groaned. Rather than let this conversation go any further astray, she turned the focus back to the book discussion. "We need to get started so we'll finish on time."

Had Kaitlyn's message been lost on Daisy? Hadn't she heard how hard it was going to be for the young mom, trying to raise her child on a minimum-wage paycheck? She'd certainly noticed her new friend's lost opportunities. Why was she saying she "couldn't wait" to have children of her own?

"Don't be in any rush," newlywed Tamera said in response to Daisy's comment. "It's hard enough trying to support a kid when both parents are working. It's gotta be twice as hard when it's just the mom taking care of everything."

Mary and the book club members had already made great strides in the past couple of weeks toward getting to know one another. Now the girls shared their stories with Daisy.

Kaitlyn, the youngest of the group, lived with her parents, who supported her emotionally but could not afford to feed an extra mouth. Thus, the need for a job. The father of the baby had an on-again, off-again relationship with Kaitlyn, and it was doubtful whether he or his parents would make an effort to help raise the child.

Eighteen-year-old Brianna's family was openly angry with her for conceiving outside of marriage and had informed her she was not welcome to stay with them after the baby was born. To make matters worse, her boyfriend had broken up with her the day after he learned she was expecting. It was clear she had nowhere to turn and was afraid of what the future might bring, but she generally kept her worries to herself. Mary made a note to mention the situation to Katina and ask if there were any services available for a girl in her position.

Chelsea's parents were big-time corporate executives, leaving Mary to assume she didn't share the others' financial worries. Her boyfriend lived near her grandmother, which was how they had met, and he was standing by her as they awaited her due date next month.

Talk turned from the financial difficulty of raising children to being out of step with classmates who can't begin to understand what expectant moms go through. Since the girls were making valid points that Mary wanted Daisy to hear, she didn't try to stop the conversation.

"The bigger you get, the less the other kids at school want to hang around with you," Brianna said. Although she had already graduated before she became pregnant, she acknowledged she had seen the difficulties an expectant classmate had experienced.

"I have great friends," Daisy said. "They accept me as I am."

If she was working so hard to change herself and conform to her friends' standards, were they truly accepting of her? Mary sighed. Regardless of what the friends thought of Daisy, she just wished her granddaughter would accept herself as the unique, charming, and creative girl that she was.

FIVE

◆◆◆

After a night of restful sleep, Mary considered the saying that when answers come in dreams, it's really just your subconscious ideas speaking to you. Of course, Mary believed the ideas had to come from somewhere, most likely from God. So when plan B bubbled up from the recesses of her mind during the night, she attributed it to God's wisdom. If He spoke to Joseph, Solomon, and biblical kings in their dreams, why wouldn't He speak to her and others of this generation the same way?

Rather than risk losing the thought by waiting until after she'd dressed for the day, she retrieved her laptop computer and sat cross-legged on the bed while she waited for the machine to boot up. A couple of minutes later, she logged on to www.annualcreditreport.com to order the free yearly documentation allowed by the Fair Credit Reporting Act. Having never requested the materials before, she was glad to see that she could get free copies of listings by the three major US credit reporting agencies: Equifax, Experian, and TransUnion.

She proceeded to provide the required information to prove that she was really whom she claimed to be and clicked the button to send the report to her e-mail account rather than via snail mail to her house. The instructions indicated that the report would be e-mailed within a few minutes, or possibly as long as a few hours, depending upon how busy the site was at that particular time.

A quick check of her e-mail revealed that it had not come through immediately, so she made a mental note to check it again later today.

She powered down the laptop and laid out a pale pink sweater and black slacks before a disturbing thought occurred to her: She had just given her personal information to a Web site she had never visited before.

"Easy, Mary," she told herself. "You found it through an official government Web site, so it's legitimate." That's what identity theft did to people; it made them paranoid about even the most innocent transfers of personal data.

Unwilling to go through life being paranoid and suspicious, she closed her eyes, released a calming breath, and asked God to protect her from further violations of her financial privacy, and to take away her burden of worry.

She'd probably have to continue turning over the burden to her heavenly Father in the future, but for now—for this moment—a sense of peace settled over her heart.

———

After commandeering so much of Henry's time yesterday, Mary couldn't bring herself to ask him for yet another ride today. If not for the icy patches on the walk between here and the bookshop, she would have hoofed it. Betty, who had made it clear that Mary could borrow her car whenever she needed, had activities scheduled for this morning—a morning in which her sister had started the day free of pain. Since Betty felt well enough to run errands and attend meetings, Mary was reluctant to impinge on her sense of independence by asking to use the car.

She slid behind the wheel of her own car and stuck the key in the ignition. Yep, the next car would definitely have seat warmers.

To her surprise and delight, the Impala started right up and ran as smoothly as it had a couple of months ago, before it first started showing signs of transmission trouble. The smooth purr of the engine gave no hint of the hiccups or whining it had been exhibiting lately, leaving her with the fleeting, fanciful thought that perhaps her car had undergone a spontaneous healing.

But then the sensible side of her kicked in and nudged her to drive it to Honest Wayne's today while it was cooperating. Even if his repair crew were to fix it right away, it could sit on his lot for a few days, or even a week or two, until she got the credit fiasco fixed and the loan straightened out and could afford to pay the bill. As for the rest of today, perhaps one of Wayne's employees would give her a ride to the shop. Then she was certain she'd be able to bum a ride home from Rebecca or ask Betty to come and pick her up at quitting time.

But before heading out in the unpredictable Impala, she went back inside to bring Gus out in his cat carrier and let her sister know where she was going. At Betty's show of concern, she promised to call if she ran into any trouble.

The car pulled smoothly out of the driveway and proceeded uneventfully through its automatic gear shifting as she headed westward toward Honest Wayne's.

Since the car was driving unbelievably well, perhaps a side trip to Ivy Bay's chamber of commerce would be in order. Besides, it was only a quarter mile out of the way, so she felt confident the car would get her there despite the short detour.

The loan officer's secretary had mentioned the fraudulent credit card had been opened at a local business. Perhaps someone at the chamber of commerce could give her a list of Ivy Bay businesses that offered credit services for their customers.

A parking spot one and a half car lengths long opened up right in front of the building, and Mary smiled at her good fortune. No circling the block to look for a space, and no zigging or zagging to maneuver the car into the parallel slot. She pulled up beside the car in front of the open area and gently shifted the car into reverse.

The Impala groaned in protest, then suddenly lurched its back end toward the opening. Mary slammed the brake for fear the momentum would propel the vehicle into the curb or, worse, into the car behind her. Slowly, she eased off the brake, and the car proceeded in a more mannerly fashion while she carefully steered it into the ample space.

She put it in park, and the engine revved of its own accord. Gus backed farther into his carrier, and his blue eyes widened at the high-pitched strain of the engine. Uncomfortable with the bizarre behavior of her formerly reliable car, Mary pulled the key from the ignition to quiet its protestations.

She fluffed the blanket in the bottom of the cat carrier and promised Gus she'd be back before the interior of the car had a chance to cool down much. The fact-finding mission at the chamber of commerce shouldn't take too long. Perhaps by the time she returned, the car would have settled down enough to make it the rest of the way to Honest Wayne's.

This time, she didn't dare hope for a spontaneous healing. But a temporary remission would certainly be nice.

Inside the more-than-a-century-old carriage house that had been converted to an office, Mary was greeted by a meager surge of heated air from the ancient furnace and a warm welcome from a middle-aged gentleman she'd met before but whose name she couldn't remember. He, on the other hand, apparently remembered her.

The man didn't bother to invite her to sit down, which was fine with her since Gus was waiting in the car, and probably working up a good pout. She'd keep the visit short.

"Good morning, Mrs. Fisher," he said. "You're just in time to place an ad in the May issue of *Ivy Bay Happenings*. There's a special section featuring our local small businesses and events." He winked, and his bushy gray eyebrow flicked like a squirrel's tail. "Better claim your space now to promote your part in the spring sidewalk sale."

He was right. It would be a good idea to advertise the books she planned to sell during the historical reenactments. "When is payment due?"

"When you reserve the space. But seeing as it's you, we can hold off until the end of March, when we finish laying out the magazine." He lifted one shoulder as if to say the decision was hers. "When you bring the ad copy, just tell Eleanor that

Edison Bentley said it's okay to turn in the payment after the ad copy."

Now she remembered. Ed was a friend of Henry's, who jokingly called him Edsel Bentley, as if the gentleman had been named after two different cars. Betty's sister-in-law Eleanor Blakely headed up the chamber of commerce, but volunteers, such as Ed, filled in occasionally as needed. His presence here today told her this must be Eleanor's day away from the office. Perhaps she and Betty were spending the morning together.

"Thank you," Mary said, and hesitated for a moment while she debated what to do.

She didn't like taking on debt, but this was an expected cost of doing business. Ideally, the money she put into the ad would come back to her many times over in sales from customers who might not otherwise stumble upon the reading treasures awaiting them at Mary's Mystery Bookshop. This was one of those times when she would have to step out in faith that, as the verse in Ecclesiastes promised, the bread she cast upon the waters would be returned to her.

She considered the decision and silently sought God's will before shaking Ed Bentley's hand to commit to a quarter-page ad in the slick, full-color magazine. It would be pricey, but her much smaller ad last year had done well, so she swallowed and sealed the deal.

They lined up how the ad would appear, and Mary promised to turn in the ad copy by the end of this month. The payment would have to wait.

"Is there anything else I can do for you?" Ed rubbed his hands together as if he relished the prospect of serving others.

"I'm not sure." Perhaps she was tilting at windmills, but when something was off center in her world, she felt obligated to set matters right, if at all possible. It wasn't in her nature to sit around and hope circumstances would right themselves without any effort on her part. "I was wondering how many of Ivy Bay's local businesses offer credit cards to their customers."

She hoped Ed wouldn't ask why she wanted such information, because she'd rather not go into all the disturbing details. And such a conversation would have been worse with Eleanor, who came from a moneyed background and might not understand the frightening little flutter that settled in Mary's chest whenever she thought of the slight-but-real possibility of having to pay off the fraudulent credit card.

"Thinking of offering credit to your bookaholics?" Ed shot Mary a thumbs-up. "Business must be doing well."

She hadn't considered such an option for her business and doubted it would offer any benefits that her customers couldn't get elsewhere. And after her recent unpleasant discovery of the bogus account, she'd really rather not go into such a venture for her shop.

"God is good," she said in answer to his second comment.

Ed tugged at one fleshy earlobe while he pondered the answer to her question. "To my knowledge, we don't keep a list of businesses that offer credit, but I can tell you my wife has a card from Cape Cod Togs. She can use it anywhere but gets extra points for purchases made at the store—one of those spend-money-to-save-money deals. Is that what you mean?"

Mary tried to cover her instinctive flinch at the thought of people actually buying into the spend-to-save mentality. Not that Ed's wife embraced that philosophy, but it certainly permeated today's culture of constant acquisition.

"Yes, that's the kind of account I'm talking about. Do you happen to recall if there are other Ivy Bay businesses that offer their own credit cards?"

Ed shook his head. "I suppose you could check at some of the high-end shops. Too bad the hardware store doesn't offer one. I'd save a bundle, considering all the tools and stuff I buy."

Mary shook his hand and thanked him for his help. It wasn't as much information as she had hoped for, but at least his suggestion offered a place to start her search to find out which business had issued a card in her name.

SIX

◆◆

Once again, the car started up fine, leading Mary to believe that she could squeeze in one more quick stop before taking it to Honest Wayne's for a new transmission. She glanced over at Gus, who had burrowed under the blanket and now refused to look at her. If he was this annoyed now, how would he feel after a second stop?

"I'll make the next errand even quicker than this one," she promised.

Gus turned his back to her and licked his shoulder as if to comfort himself.

Mary rolled her eyes at his theatrics.

Cape Cod Togs wasn't far. If she timed everything right, she could check to see if the upscale clothing boutique had issued a credit card in her name, drive the Impala to Honest Wayne's, and catch a ride back to the bookshop in under thirty minutes.

She took care shifting into drive and proceeded at a steady pace to prevent unnecessary gear changes in the automatic transmission. The car purred like a cream-fed cat.

But after a half mile, the whining sound started up again.

"Come on, I know you can make it." She patted the steering wheel as if that were enough to encourage the car to continue on despite its ailment.

The light turned yellow, and she coasted to an easy stop. Unfortunately, the car's protestations continued. Perhaps she should reconsider making the extra stop at Cape Cod Togs today. She needed answers so she could stop further purchases from being made in her name, but the greater need at the moment was to avoid being stranded on the road.

But before she could decide whether the risk of a breakdown exceeded the potential advantage of stopping at Cape Cod Togs, the Impala revved high again and followed with a bang and a thump. Gus backed farther into his crate and expressed his displeasure with a low yowl.

Mary wasn't a mechanic, but it sounded to her ears as if something had fallen out of the car. Worse, the car refused to move. Rather than risk further damage to the engine, she switched off the key in the ignition and blew out a breath of frustration.

The light turned green, and the person in the car behind her tooted a reminder to go.

With the engine shut off, the electric window wouldn't roll down, so she opened the door slightly, stuck out her hand, and waved for them to go around. A gust of cold New England air swept through the interior and seemed to suck out the warmth that the heater had pumped in until a minute ago.

Ever the optimist, Mary tried the ignition again, hopeful that the previous purr would return. This time, the transmission screamed as if it were preparing for a space launch.

"Never mind that," she conceded and switched the engine off, for good this time. Now she pressed the car's four-way flasher button and retrieved the cell phone from her purse.

Gus rocked his carrier, clearly upset over the unfamiliar sounds and annoyed with the delay.

Mary pulled out the business card she'd been given yesterday and punched in the numbers that would connect her directly to the person who could help her.

"Hello, Wayne? It looks like I'll need that tow truck after all."

———

Fortunately for Mary, Cape Cod Togs was within easy walking distance from the shop, across the street from the clerk's office on Meeting House Road. Since she'd already missed time from work this morning, she'd encouraged Rebecca to take her lunchtime first. After her employee returned from the Black & White Diner, Mary hoofed it around the corner to the clothing store that Ed Bentley had mentioned offered credit cards for its customers.

On entering the exclusive boutique, it felt as though she were entering another world altogether. A world of decadent quality, a soothing environment that invited customers to linger, and intuitive clerks who understood when to let folks shop uninterrupted and when to offer help.

Waxed cherry floors gleamed under soft light that radiated from recessed fixtures in the ceiling, the scent of eucalyptus and mint wafted through the spacious showroom, and racks of attractive clothing were spaced out in a manner that invited shoppers to mix and match tops, bottoms, and accessories. Upholstered chairs were clustered near a trio of mirrors where, presumably, husbands could sit while their wives shopped, and perhaps offer an opinion on the outfits their ladies tried on.

Apparently deducing that Mary could use some help, Carolee Benson approached and asked if there was something in particular Mary was looking for. The talented clerk was known to her, not because she shopped here routinely, but because Mary had come here with Betty once to have a dress fitted. The store was a bit out of her price range for everyday wear, but it seemed like the kind of place a hard-charging credit rustler might shop. Because if a person could shop to his or her heart's content without having to worry about paying for the elite items they coveted, why would they go to a bargain store?

"Are you looking for weekend wear, or perhaps something for a special event?" Carolee asked, her voice as soft and peaceful as the classical music piped through the store's speakers.

Mary didn't want to go into the whole story about the credit card, but she didn't want to be deceptive either. Perhaps *vague* would be appropriate for the circumstances.

"I'm here to inquire about a credit card that was opened recently. I was wondering if you could check your records and tell me if there's a balance."

Carolee pulled a long face, as if she were more disappointed by the news she was about to share than Mary would be. "I'm so sorry, but we don't have access to the account after it's opened. All I can do is run your card through for a sale and tell you whether it's accepted or declined."

"I see." Mary wrung her hands, wondering what the next step might be. It looked as though it was time to come up with a plan C, or even D.

"Or if you'd rather, I can check your points balance to see how many Tog Tags you've acquired from your previous purchases."

"Tog Tags?"

"Yes, you get a tag for every hundred dollars you spend. Then you can use them at the store, same as cash. Each one is worth ten dollars."

"How clever." A 10 percent discount might not necessarily draw customers into the store, but same-as-cash coupons for devoted shoppers was an excellent way to get those big spenders back in the store. She would give some thought to offering a similar plan for her bookstore customers. It all depended on how much work such a strategy would entail.

"You would have been signed up for the Tog Tag program when you opened your credit account. I can look you up by entering your name to see how many points you have." Carolee moved to the cash register and punched some keys. "Do you spell Fisher with a *c* or without?"

Unwilling to waste the woman's time, Mary started to ask her not to bother. But on second thought, she realized that the information could tell her approximately how much had been spent in the store over the past month or so. And if there had been any transactions, perhaps she could ask a manager to check the store's security tapes on the dates the purchases were made.

Mary smiled, heartened at the possibility that her identity thief's image might have been caught on tape.

"Without a *c*," she said.

Fingers flew, and Carolee leaned in to stare at the screen, a perplexed expression covering her features. "That's weird. I'm not finding you in the system."

Mary leaned in, on the unlikely possibility she might be able to see what the store clerk could not. But, no, not a single Fisher, or even a Fischer, graced the list of Tog Tag earners.

Which meant only one thing. The identity thief had not registered for the credit card from this store.

Mary groaned as she considered how many Ivy Bay businesses she'd have to comb through to find out which one of them had issued the credit card. She could almost hear the constant ringing of cash registers as the thief continued merrily on with his or her shopping spree.

———

The free credit report still hadn't come through by the time the midweek church service began that evening. Mary slipped into the pew beside Betty and Daisy. Across the aisle, Henry sat next to Jill Sanderson, her husband, Harry, and their two rambunctious boys who clearly wanted Henry's undivided attention. He nodded a hello as she settled next to her family.

Dorothy turned in the row in front of her and, noticing Henry's nod in their direction, smiled broadly and gave a little finger wave. But when he turned away, clearly not having noticed her greeting, her smile abruptly disappeared. She clamped her lips together and faced forward, saying not a word to Mary.

Betty laid a hand on Mary's knee and offered a gentle smile. She didn't have to say anything. Mary knew her sister had witnessed the bit of testiness that had just played out.

Pastor Miles stepped up to the podium and directed them to open their Bibles. Wednesday night services were usually shorter and more casual than Sunday morning sermons. And the pastor often tried to make the midweek message relevant to what was happening in the world. Tonight, he delivered a moving Valentine's message. First, he focused on the importance of friendship as the base for a successful romance. Next, he talked about mutual submission between husbands and wives and the power of each sacrificing their will for the other so that God's will can rule. And finally, he brought home the significance of God's love in all relationships, both platonic and romantic.

"God loves you." Pastor Miles cast his gaze over the audience, meeting their eyes as if willing them to understand that God's love was personal to each and every one of them. "He loves you exactly as you are right this very minute."

Mary leaned forward slightly and peered out of the corner of her eye to see if the message was making an impression on Daisy. The girl sat with her head down and picked at a spot of nail polish on her cuticle. Mary remembered how her own children had often appeared as if they weren't taking in a word that was spoken, either at church or when she gave them motherly advice. Later, when she least expected it, they had surprised her by mentioning information she assumed had fallen on deaf ears. Now she hoped that, like her children had done in the past, Daisy was hearing the message that seemed custom-made for her.

Pastor Miles led them in an a cappella rendition of "Just As I Am" and closed with a short prayer.

"That was his best Valentine's Day sermon ever," Betty said. "And he never even used the old standby—First Corinthians, chapter thirteen."

"Quite impressive," Mary agreed.

The congregation started to rise, but Pastor Miles urged them back to their seats. "I'm sorry for the delay, but I was just reminded of an important announcement."

He went on to explain that the upcoming Winter Carnival, to be held this weekend at Albert Paddington Park, was being held to benefit the health clinic and urged all in attendance to go, have a good time, and spend their money for a good cause.

"The activities committee of our church has made an excellent suggestion that we host an information booth in the park to invite people to attend our services. Let them know God loves them, and that we do too. We need volunteers to man the booth and pass out pamphlets. Friday is covered by Dorothy Johnson and other committee members, but we could use more volunteers on Saturday."

Considering the purpose of the Winter Carnival was to help people who needed affordable health care, Mary considered it a great idea to also share God's love and acceptance with those who also needed spiritual care.

Her hand automatically went up, and Pastor Miles acknowledged her with a nod and a quiet thank-you. Betty grinned at her easy willingness to help. What could she say? It was for a worthy cause and, as a bonus, it was a great way to socialize with people in the community.

Dorothy turned sideways in her seat and slanted a cursory glance in her direction. The serious-natured woman was involved in numerous activities in the church and seemed to consider it her duty to keep everything running smoothly. Mary doubted Dorothy could be more involved if she cloned herself.

A moment later, Henry's hand went up. This time, the gesture was followed quickly by Dorothy's upraised hand and a quick explanation. "I'll be at the carnival on Saturday, anyway, so I may as well help out."

With that, Dorothy turned to Mary and lifted her chin as if to say, "Don't think you're getting him all to yourself."

Mary didn't have time to consider what had prompted that response, because Daisy lifted her hand and said, "I'll babysit for the volunteers who need it."

Sometimes, as when Daisy pretended to be someone she was not, she seemed so very young. And then there were times like tonight, when the girl recognized a potential need and offered her services, that made Mary realize just how quickly her granddaughter was growing up. A sense of grandmotherly pride threatened to burst the buttons on her blouse.

On their way out, single folks, young and old, were talking about the upcoming Cupid Couples matchups to be announced at the Winter Carnival on Friday. Some speculated who might be paired together, and others claimed that the benefit of the matchup was to meet someone altogether new.

On urging from Betty, Mary had filled out her questionnaire, enclosed the entry fee, and given it to Jada, the secretary for the Cupid committee. Mary still didn't feel comfortable putting herself "out there" as Daisy had phrased it, but she agreed it was time to take a little risk, to be open to a new relationship, if that's what God had in store for her. However, doing what she felt was right, and liking it, were two different things.

Lynn Teagarden, a prayer group member, sidled up to her as she stepped out into the church aisle. The tall, slender mother of two teens was as opposite from Mary as one could imagine, but their differences were part of what made them find each other so interesting.

"Thanks for offering to help out on Saturday," said Lynn. "I'm coordinating the volunteer schedules, so I'd like to pencil you in from noon to two, if that's all right with you."

"Sure thing. I'm happy to help."

The dark-haired woman frowned, making it clear something was troubling her.

"What's up?" Mary prodded.

Lynn paused a moment, clearly considering whether she should share her concern. After a moment's hesitation, she stepped out of the aisle.

Mary joined her in an empty pew and told Betty and Daisy that she would catch up with them in a few minutes.

Lynn lowered her voice. "I don't like to share gossip, and I wouldn't ordinarily say anything, but I recently heard whispers about something that concerns me." She paused before continuing. "It involves your friend Katina, from the health clinic."

"Is something wrong? Anything I can do?" She didn't know Katina well, but if there was a need she could fill, she would be happy to do so.

"I don't know exactly what the situation is," Lynn said, "but talk is that there has been some kind of impropriety or violation on the Cupid committee, and Katina is at the center of it."

Mary considered the information—or noninformation, as the case may be—that was being shared with her. Since Lynn wasn't sure what the offense might be, Mary wasn't going to rush to any conclusions.

"I brought the matter up with Dorothy, but she was adamant that she didn't want to talk about it." Lynn looked down at the Bible in her hand. "Her reaction kind of made me feel like a two-bit gossip, but that truly wasn't my intent."

A few rows away, Henry said his good-byes to the Sanderson boys with a complicated move of fist bumps and high fives, then stepped out into the aisle. He made eye contact with Mary and headed toward her. Before he got very far, Dorothy intercepted him, smiled coyly, and touched his hand like a schoolgirl waiting to be asked to the homecoming dance.

"I believe you," Mary said. Her friend was aware of much that went on in Ivy Bay and had proved time and again that she could be trusted with even the most sensitive of secrets. Lynn was not the kind of person who took joy in trotting out other people's transgressions. Something about Katina's alleged impropriety was troubling her friend, and she suspected Lynn only brought it up now because she needed either advice or a sounding board. Possibly both.

"Thank you. I knew you'd understand. Anyway, I was concerned that the Cupid situation be handled appropriately, especially since the church is staffing a booth at the event."

She paused as if struggling for the right words to voice her fears without making any outright accusations. "Katina is the registrar for the Cupid Couples matchups. I understand an audit of her portion of the Cupid committee's procedures is being conducted."

Mary closed her eyes and wished away the suggestion that had just been made. When she opened them again, Lynn still stood before her, clearly waiting for a response that would help her decide what to do with the unpleasant snippet of information that had fallen into her lap. Unfortunately, out of sight and out of mind didn't work in this situation.

Worse, her mind now dredged up the offhand comment Katina had made when telling her about the impending arrival of baby number four. The nurse had clearly been concerned about the financial impact the new baby would have on her family, especially at a time when she was already struggling to find the resources to register her oldest child for college.

As the person who had collected the fees along with the Cupid Couples applications, might Katina have been tempted to misappropriate those funds? To divert them to her own pocket to help with mounting personal expenses? Worse, as head of the entire Winter Carnival fund-raising event, Katina had access to all the cash that would come in this weekend from vendor sales and last-minute entry fees. With so much at stake, Mary considered it prudent—not gossipy—of Lynn to mention her concern.

But she was getting ahead of herself. "Let's not jump to conclusions," she said, as much to herself as to Lynn. "There may be a perfectly reasonable explanation for the audit. We don't want to sound the alert without just cause. But that doesn't mean we shouldn't keep our eyes and ears open. In the meantime, I'll make a few subtle inquiries and see what I can find out next time I'm at the clinic."

Lynn smiled and rubbed a hand over her Bible as if assuring herself that Mary's suggestion was a solid one. "I knew you would come up with the right thing to do. If not for the church's involvement, and of course the needs of the clinic patients at stake, I would have just kept my misgivings to myself."

"Well, you did the right thing. I'll let you know if I learn of anything that needs to be brought to light."

With that, Lynn scooted out into the aisle and caught up with her family. By now, Henry had disengaged from Dorothy and made his way to Mary. He greeted her with a smile, and they walked toward the exit together.

"The weather forecast is iffy for tomorrow morning, so I'm going to wait until later to take my boat out and test the new motor," he said. "If you need a ride to the bookshop, I'm happy to be at your service."

"That's so sweet of you to offer. I would be charmed to ride with you."

Henry laughed, his deep voice carrying through the church.

At that moment, Dorothy stiff-armed her way around Mary. "Now, Henry, don't forget. I'll see you at the Cupid matchup on Friday," she said, her voice syrupy sweet. For Mary, she granted only a curt nod before she scurried out the door.

Mary grinned at the man who managed to capture the attention of many females with his good looks and courteous manner. "A date?"

He shook his head. "Nah. She was telling me she had registered for the Cupid thing and thought it would be funny if we got paired together."

The Cupid thing? "You mean you—"

A sheepish grin stole across his face. "My grandkids pestered me until I agreed to sign up. I'm not expecting anything from it. I just consider the entry fee a charitable donation."

She nodded her agreement, but a troubling thought whispered from the back of her mind. The question was, whose charity—the health clinic or the college fund for Katina's eldest?

SEVEN

Mary opened the e-mail program on the shop's computer and checked to see if she'd received a report back from the credit bureau. She had filled out the online application a couple of days ago, after making no headway with the loan company that had delivered the news about the rogue credit card showing up in her records.

Nope. Nothing. Just a couple of spam messages that had slipped past her junk-mail filtering system. One offered her a full head of thick hair and the other an at-home job that could earn her a six-figure income, but only if she was among the first to respond. She clicked the Delete button and removed them from her in-box.

Odd. The free annual credit report was supposed to come instantly via the Internet, which was why she had chosen that method of delivery.

The waiting was driving her crazy. She needed to do something, anything, to stay busy and keep her mind off the excruciating delay.

The bell over the door rang again, and a family entered in search of stories for young readers. Rebecca welcomed them and led them to the area of the store where the children's mysteries were shelved.

Mary redirected her attention to the pile of traded books that sat on the counter, waiting to be inventoried and shelved for sale. She picked up a pile of books and carried them to a clear area of the checkout counter to sort through them. The process gave her an interesting peek into her customers' interests, and she was often surprised to discover how their books met or defied her assumptions. This scary thriller had been turned in by an older woman who was so shy she barely said boo whenever she came into the shop. A burly, outdoorsy-looking man had traded in these cozies. The ones that actually fit the stereotype were the technological suspense novels brought in by a teenage boy, the self-professed geek who sometimes showed up at the shop just in time to answer a computer question or two.

She stacked those books and moved on to the small pile Wayne had brought in. On the top sat *Raising the Stakes*, another in the Las Vegas mystery series. In this case, it sort of fit. She supposed that every time a potential customer walked onto his car lot, there was the chance they'd walk away without a sale. But, like the main character in this book, Wayne always clung to the possibility that the next customer would be his jackpot.

As she'd done with the other paperbacks, Mary riffled the pages to check the condition of the paper and binding.

Rebecca returned from the back of the shop. "You dropped something." She picked it up and handed it to Mary.

The scrap of paper that had fallen from between the book's pages turned out to be a prescription refill for ropinirole, made out for Wayne Chapman. In her time at the bookstore, she had seen more unusual things used as bookmarks: a piece of tree bark, a lock of hair, candy wrappers, feathers, a crumb-filled muffin wrapper that probably came from the bakery next door, a four-leaf clover, and even an ultrasound photo of an unborn baby.

She took the prescription to the lost-and-found box behind the counter for safekeeping until the next time she saw Wayne, then thought better of it. A prescription was very personal, and he might not like it if others were able to see his private medical information. So she stuck the slip in an envelope, wrote his name on the outside, and placed it in a drawer.

"You go home and get ready for the Winter Carnival," Rebecca said. "I'll close up shop." As an afterthought, she winked in amusement at what Cupid mischief must be in store for Mary tonight.

Ashley was at home with her father, and Daisy had stayed home with Betty to do some chores, so they weren't here to help. But business was slow to moderate, and Rebecca should be able to handle the work flow. If Mary left now, she could go home, have an early dinner, and head to the park in plenty of time for the Cupid Couples public pairings. Two out of three weren't bad.

She pushed a hand through her gray curls. "I'd rather stay here."

"And miss out on a date with the man of your dreams?" Rebecca waved her toward the door. "Go now, while the getting is good."

"My expectations are obviously not as high as yours."

"Oh, where's your sense of fun? Go. Have a good time." Her assistant handed Mary her purse, coat, and kitty carrier. "I'll want to hear all about it later," Rebecca insisted.

"Thanks, Rebecca. I think." Mary put Gus in his carrier and pulled on her coat.

Her cell phone rang, so she set the carrier back down and looked at the caller ID. Another call from the mortgage company. Would this call offer more nonanswers today? Her hopes deflated even before taking the call, she clicked the Talk button and asked God to bless the conversation.

This time it was Mrs. Hamblen. Judging by her congested cough, the secretary had actually understated Mrs. Hamblen's condition.

"Oh my," said Mary. "You really *are* sick."

"If you think this is wonderful, you should have heard me earlier this week."

That was a treat Mary could live without.

Mrs. Hamblen apologized for taking so long to get back to her.

"I'm just glad you're feeling a little better." Glad, as well, to hear from someone who could give her actual answers. Even so, Mary thought her loan officer might have been better off if she had continued recuperating throughout the weekend.

Mrs. Hamblen tapped computer keys to pull up the loan information, and Mary realized she was squeezing the phone. She flexed her fingers and waited for the verdict.

In the next few minutes, Mary was finally privy to what little information the company had—the name of the credit card company, the account number, and a toll-free phone number.

"That's all I have, but at least it gives you a place to start," said the loan officer. "I know you're anxious to get this cleared up so we can move forward with your loan."

Mary thanked her for the information, hung up, and checked her watch. It was getting late, but she needed to call now, even if it made her late for the carnival.

She took off her coat and moved away from the checkout register while she keyed in the requested identifying information. None of the recorded options offered what she was looking for, so she pressed the key to be connected to an operator.

First, she explained that a rogue card had been opened under her name, but the person on the other end didn't seem interested. Instead, the young-sounding guy stuck to the script in front of him: Name. Address. Account number again, even though she had already keyed that information in. Last four digits of her Social Security number. The operator took an inordinate amount of time keying the information in, leaving Mary to guess he might be new at his job.

"And what is your mother's maiden name?"

"Randlett."

"I'm sorry; that's not it."

Her frustration starting to mount, Mary flexed her fingers again to release some of the tension. The loan officer's secretary had naively suggested that a typo might have been the cause of having this card added to Mary's credit record, so maybe a typo was responsible for the maiden name glitch. "Try spelling it with one *t*."

Computer keys clacked. "No, that doesn't work either. Are you sure that's the correct name?"

Mary pulled the phone from her ear and stared at it. *Patience, Mary.* She put the phone back to her ear. "Yes, I'm sure. It's the name on my mother's birth certificate, her death certificate, and lots of official papers in between. So yes, I'm very sure."

"Well, someone obviously made a mistake." The implication in the customer service operator's voice pointed to Mary.

"Can you at least tell me the balance? I need to know how big a problem I'm dealing with."

"I'm sorry. I can't give you that information without proper identification."

"This is turning into a 'Who's on First?' routine."

"A what?"

"Abbott and Costello." Silence. "The comedians?"

More silence. Then, "Is there anything else I can help you with today?"

Hmm. The young man on the phone might consider this matter closed, but she sure didn't. Since he had confirmed that her name and address matched that on the account, this clearly wasn't a simple mistake involving transposed account numbers. "Yes, I'd like to close the account and report it as fraudulent."

"I can't do that, ma'am."

By now, Mary was pacing the floor. Gus watched from the cat carrier, his pale blue eyes tracking the path of her shoes. "Why not?"

"For one, you can't prove you are the credit card holder."

"Because I didn't open the account?"

"Right."

Aaarrrggghhh! Could this ridiculous process be any more frustrating? She pasted on a smile in the hope it would prevent her annoyance from coming through in her words. "And what's the other reason?"

"Well, because I've never handled a disputed account before."

"Couldn't you at least flag it with an alert or something?" It wasn't her place to teach the young man his job, but *something* needed to be done.

"Maybe I should let you speak with my supervisor."

She wished she had suggested that right from the beginning.

Rebecca caught her eye and lifted a thumb to ask if all was going smoothly.

With regret and a tiny remaining shred of optimism, Mary tilted her head and shrugged one shoulder. "Yes," she said into the phone, "a supervisor would be a good idea."

Unfortunately, she had to go through the entire process all over again with the supervisor. Account number, card holder's name and address, last four digits of the Social Security number, and the holdup: her mother's maiden name. Same information in, same nonanswers.

"I'm sorry," said the woman on the other end of the line. "That maiden name is not letting us in."

"Yes, that's why I was connected to you." She went through the whole deal again, about how the account had been opened without her knowledge or permission.

"Maybe it's just a reporting error," the woman said, unhelpfully echoing the opinions of others in an obvious but futile attempt to ease her fears.

"Regardless of how it came to be," Mary said, speaking slowly to make herself completely understood, "at the very least, it's affecting my credit rating. At worst, I may be stuck paying for purchases I never made."

"Oh, so you're saying someone made unauthorized purchases to your account?"

Not her account, but she was getting tired of arguing the point. "Yes, unauthorized purchases were made."

"Good, we can do something about that. I'll flag the account, which will freeze the card so no new purchases can be made. Then it'll go to the fraud department who will contact you within the next seven to ten business days."

"What about the balance?" When the loan officer's secretary had broken the news to her about the credit problem, she had cited the frequency of use and high balance as cause for putting the loan on hold. "I was told I may need to make the minimum payments until the matter is cleared up, but I can't afford to pay it."

"If the purchases are found to be fraudulent, you won't be held accountable for any continuing charges on the account," the woman assured her, "but we'll have to look into the nature of the individual charges to see if you're liable for any of those."

That was a start, but it wasn't exactly what Mary wanted to hear. A lot of charges had already piled up. Until she could sort things out and prove she did not buy those items, she would be responsible for making at least the minimum payment when the bill came due.

"In the meantime," the supervisor continued, "I can tell you which bank issued the card. If you go to their office and show your identification, they may be able to give you more information."

Finally! A scrap of hope. Perhaps there was a way out of this mess after all.

She thanked the woman profusely, grabbed the cat carrier, rushed out to the car she'd borrowed from Betty this morning, and arrived at the bank six minutes too late. Despite the fact that she knew it was closed, she got out of the car and walked to the entrance. Inside, tellers were finishing up their end-of-day duties. One looked up and, noticing Mary with one hand on the unbudging door, pointed at her watch and shook her head.

Mary waved to acknowledge the unwelcome message that she'd have to wait until Monday to talk to someone, face-to-face. No matter how this unfortunate predicament turned out, she knew one thing for sure.

She was going to have to be her own advocate.

EIGHT

---◆◆◆---

Mary's nerves were still buzzing when she, Betty, and Daisy arrived at the Winter Carnival. She wasn't sure of the cause: Was it the credit card situation or the impending unveiling of her Cupid date? All she knew was that she wanted both of them over and done with, posthaste.

Outside the reception hall, a few twentysomething guys egged on one of their group to ride the mechanical bull. Farther away, a riding lawn mower, masquerading as a train engine, pulled tot-size cars carrying tot-size passengers inside an area cordoned off with a portable fence. A couple of mothers walked beside the slow-moving choo-choo to make sure the precious cargo remained seated. In a quieter area, away from the main foot traffic, a sign perched beside a straw-littered paddock promised pony rides starting tomorrow morning at eleven o'clock. And then there was the attention-grabbing WIVY roving radio van.

"The radio station has been advertising the carnival all week," said Betty. She turned and peered back at the mostly full parking lot. "Looks like people have been listening."

Inside, they were greeted by a welcome burst of warm air and the amplified voice of the radio deejay introducing an

Elvis impersonator. "For our listeners at home, why aren't you here? You're about to miss an incredible entertainer. Come on down to Albert Paddington Park until ten o'clock tonight and see for yourselves all the fun activities in store for you."

They checked their coats just inside the door—a clever ploy to increase donation dollars for the clinic—and headed toward the source of the noise.

Multitasking to the max, the deejay cut to a recorded song to go out over the airwaves, turned off the volume for the in-person audience, and handed the stage mic to the Elvis with the bad wig.

"Elvis?" Daisy said. "Really?"

Mary wasn't about to say so, but she agreed with her granddaughter's surprise over the quirky choice of entertainer. Other than the uneven wig, the man looked pretty close to the real McCoy, but his voice was noticeably pitchy. However, that didn't stop a couple of middle-aged ladies from trying to outdo each other with their own leg-twitch moves in imitation of the famed singer.

"I smell food," Mary said. Maybe one of the vendors was selling peanuts glazed with burned sugar. She turned to go in search of the Boston-named treat when Betty called her back.

"This is where they'll announce the Cupid Couples." Betty led them closer to the stage where the wannabe singer tried to hit notes just out of his reach.

Mary paused, and Daisy, who had been gawking at all the sights—and possibly keeping a lookout for cute boys— bumped into her. "Oops, sorry."

Her mind on the public Valentine drama that was about to transpire, Mary barely heard her granddaughter. A disturbing thought occurred to her. "They're not going to announce the couples on the radio, are they?"

Daisy grabbed Mary's hand. "I'm going to get some ice cream and walk around."

"Don't go far," she and Betty said in unison. Okay, so maybe a little on the protective side, but better safe than sorry.

Betty sidled closer to the stage for a better view. "Of course they're going to announce it all on the radio. And the names of the couples will be published in tomorrow's *Ivy Bay Bugle*. It's all good publicity for the clinic."

Mary removed her glasses and rubbed the heel of her hand against her eyes, as if that would erase the vision of public embarrassment that had planted itself in her mind. "If I had known that, I wouldn't have signed up."

"I know." Betty smiled, the expression sweet and unassuming. "Oh, look. There's Henry." She waved and called him over.

When he joined them, Mary blurted her anxiety by projecting it onto him. "You nervous about the Cupid Couples reveal?" She knew that was what she was doing because she'd just finished reading a mystery involving a psychologist who solved crimes by psychoanalyzing the suspects' motives.

"Nah, what's to be nervous about?"

It shouldn't have surprised her that Henry was fine with the idea of going out with a total stranger. After all, he was quite personable and found it easy to socialize with just about everyone. But Mary had assumed he'd share her discomfort over the fact that it was a *date*. Then again, maybe he hadn't tried to anticipate how the match might turn out, as she had.

"Well, suppose you're fixed up with someone who monopolizes the conversation?" she said.

He answered with a grin. "It's just one date."

This was true. And if she was truly uncomfortable about getting together with someone, one-on-one, she supposed she could find another couple to accompany them and make it a double date.

She glanced down at her watch. It wouldn't be long until what she had come to think of as the hour of doom. Her mind now firmly wedged on unpleasant thoughts, it looped back to recent events. What if her date stole her credit card when she wasn't looking?

Okay, now she felt a little foolish, and Henry's knowing gaze gave the impression that he'd been privy to her silly supposition. She pinched her arm as a physical reminder to forget about the credit card for now and just live in the moment.

"You can't be this worked up over a silly date," Henry said. "What else is bothering you?"

By now, Betty had turned away and was pointing out the location of the bathrooms for Jill Sanderson and her two boys.

Mary had already updated her sister about today's attempts to straighten out the credit card problem. Now she gave Henry a quick rundown.

He laid a hand on her shoulder and gave a comforting squeeze. "Hang in there, my friend. Truth shall prevail. You've just got to be more stubborn than the one who hijacked your ID."

He was right. She needed to persevere. How fortunate she was to have a friend like Henry. It wasn't so much *what* he said as the calm certainty with which he delivered the words. He was always like that. Seldom rattled. Almost always serene. She briefly wondered if staying out on the boat all day rocked him to a place of serenity. But then she recalled he'd always been this way, even as a child.

She reached up and patted his hand where it still rested on her shoulder.

Like a chill wind, Dorothy breezed through the crowd and made her way toward them. The stalwart woman smiled at Henry, looking neither left nor right as she approached her target. She wore that same look of determination that she used when organizing church activities. In the next moment, she singled him out from the group like a cowboy cutting a calf from the herd. Dorothy straightened the pearls at her neck, positioned herself squarely between Henry and Mary, and started telling him a story about people Mary didn't know.

Betty grabbed her arm. "Tess Bailey is selling ice cream. Let's go see if she has any of your honey ice cream left."

Bailey's Ice Cream Shop sat on the other side of Main Street from Mary's Mystery Bookshop. Shortly after Mary moved to Ivy Bay, she had become enamored of their homemade ice cream. As an ice-cream lover who owned her own ice-cream machine and enjoyed creating new recipes, she could appreciate Tess's careful selection of flavorful ingredients, the delicate balance of flavors, and marketing savvy of matching the right flavor to the right season.

She soon became friends with the owner, and one thing led to another. Before she knew it, she'd been asked to provide recipes for different ice-cream flavors to be featured every month. Happy to share her fun concoctions with Bailey's customers, Mary obliged. February's flavor, in recognition of Valentine's Day, was honey ice cream. To drive home the Valentine theme, Tess had topped the concoction with heart-shaped chocolate sprinkles.

"I've already eaten more than my share of that particular recipe, but I could go for a nice cup of hot chocolate." She gave her sister a sideways glance. "With a dollop of mint ice cream added for good measure."

When they returned a short while later with treats in hand, Dorothy was still talking. Henry, being the good-natured gentleman that he was, listened politely. On noticing their return, he moved aside to include them in their circle. Dorothy's broad smile fell flat.

"They've already started the age eighteen-to-nineteen group," he said. "Next up are the twenty to twenty-fours."

It would be a little while before the sixtysomethings' turn.

On stage, Katina, Jada, and a couple of others on the Cupid committee took turns calling out the names of matches. Each pair responded differently, some shyly shrinking in the limelight and others laughing it up and adding a party atmosphere.

If she hadn't been dreading the sound of her own name being called, Mary probably would have enjoyed the fun a lot more. She took a few deep breaths and tried to relax the tension that had settled into her shoulder muscles. It wouldn't do to panic and run away the stage when her turn came. Who knew how many other potential pair-ups were as nervous as she? Such a response could incite a stampede of other nervous singles exiting the building in a panicked crush. Imagine tomorrow's headlines. She smiled in spite of herself at her creative catastrophizing.

On a more serious note, if she merely ducked out the side door, she'd leave behind a disappointed gentleman who very likely would be embarrassed at being stood up so publicly. No, she couldn't do that to her would-be match. It would be much better to keep her jittery nerves to herself and act as if she were having a good time.

"Muscle through, Mary," she mumbled under her breath.

Beside her, Henry's booming laughter broke into her thoughts. Onstage, an attractive couple with highly extroverted personalities pretended they'd each rather have been matched with someone else. The young woman playfully batted her eyelashes at Elvis and ran her fingers through his hair, which tilted the wig to an even odder angle than it had already been. And the young man tugged at Katina's hand, led her through a goofy box-step dance, and made as if to leave the stage with this very pregnant woman instead of his selected date.

The crowd roared. After those two had posed for pictures and left the stage, Mary and many others were convinced theirs was a perfect matchup.

By the time the announcers got to Mary's age group, she was starting to wish she hadn't finished the ice-cream-adorned hot chocolate. The more names they called, the more her stomach flip-flopped.

Jada called out the next name. "Dorothy Johnson! Come on up here. And watch your step."

Dorothy beamed and pressed her hand to Katina's. Then she scanned the crowd as if wondering who her match might be. She looked so eager. So happy. Her gaze landed on Henry, and she smiled so hard her Valentine-red lipstick smeared across her teeth.

If Mary were closer, she'd hand her a napkin to wipe off the red blur. Instead, she pantomimed wiping her own teeth with her fingers, but Dorothy didn't see it. The woman's eyes were lasered to Henry.

Jada raised the mic to her mouth. "And your Cupid Couples match is...Robert Hiller!"

A spotlight scanned the crowd and landed on the postal carrier who looked as if he'd just won one of those million-dollar sweepstakes he sometimes delivered to the patrons on his route. Bob practically flew up the steps.

As he approached Dorothy, he bowed like Prince Charming before Cinderella at the ball, courteously took her hand, and led her to the photo area. Dorothy stiffened up and fingered the pearls at her neck. But after a moment, she plastered on an awkward smile for the camera, a clear effort to hide her disappointment. Though she wasn't fully successful, she deserved kudos for trying.

Bob, on the other hand, didn't seem to notice her lackluster reaction. Rather, he acted as though he'd just knocked down all the milk bottles to take home the best carnival prize ever.

Mary didn't blame him for his enthusiasm. The relentlessly formal Dorothy was actually quite attractive in her always-put-together way. Her ramrod posture made her seem a bit formidable at times, but whenever she smiled, a warmth shone through that wasn't always visible when she had her mind set on accomplishing a task, which was most of the time.

Bob, the ever-happy Main Street mail carrier, was seemingly her exact opposite. Of medium height and build, the man's shoulders rounded as if he were carrying an invisible mail pouch. And whereas Dorothy was primarily task oriented, people-loving Bob was always happy to stop work for a moment and chitchat with the customers on his route.

Katina took the mic and blew into it. "Next up is... Mary Fisher!" She smiled at Mary and applauded with the rest of the audience.

Mary remained rooted where she stood. The moment of doom had finally arrived, and she still wasn't ready for it.

Henry gave her a little nudge to jostle her out of her daze. When she was slow to move, he took her elbow and assisted her up the steps to the stage.

If Dorothy's smile had been fake, Mary's must now look absolutely plastic. She couldn't help it. She looked for her sister—her rock—but Betty was preoccupied with wiping chocolate off her hand.

Next, her gaze landed on Henry, who smiled easily, and his calm assurance reminded her this was just for fun. And to stop taking this Cupid date so seriously.

Then Katina called a familiar name.

It didn't register at first. So when Henry stepped up on the stage to join her, her confused mind supposed he was there to escort her offstage. Her knight in shining armor, coming to rescue her from the dreaded date.

Jill Sanderson and the boys started the audience in hollering and cheering, and that's when Mary realized her Cupid "date" was Henry.

Relief flooded over her like waves over Little Neck Beach during a nor'easter storm.

He stopped in front of her, and with significantly less theatricality than Bob Hiller's approach, he quietly took her hand and raised it to his lips for a chaste kiss.

His easy and casual reaction to their pairing released all the pent-up anxiety that had grown in her over the past couple of hours. When she finally unwound and gave him a smile—a real one, not the uneasy grimace she had tried to pass off as a smile—he drew her toward him and led her through a twirl. To the delight of the crowd, they hammed it up for the camera.

By now, Mary had forgotten her anxiety, and she laughed as Henry twirled her again, this time ending in a dip. They held the pose for the camera and added Bob Fosse jazz hands to the ballroom move for a grand finale.

The audience exploded with applause, and cameras flashed. By the time they were ready to leave the stage, a flashbulb haze clouded her vision, and she stumbled uneasily toward the steps. Henry swiftly grasped her arm to steady her as she cautiously made her way down.

Dorothy walked by, Bob trotting happily at her heels. Flashbulb eyes or not, Mary wasn't too blinded by the cameras to catch Dorothy giving her the stink eye.

NINE

◆◆◆

Mary and Henry were quickly swallowed up in hugs and back claps. She couldn't begin to measure her relief at not having to go on a date with a stranger. She should have followed her own instincts and refrained from registering for the Cupid matchup. One thing was for sure: She would definitely remember this the next time she felt pressed to do something that, deep down inside, didn't feel quite right to her.

Looking up at Henry, who beamed at all those around him, she supposed God had saved her from her own hasty decision. There was no doubt she'd have a blast in Henry's company. Surprised, relieved, and happy, she gave silent thanks to God for sparing her from a potentially uncomfortable meeting with a stranger who might have been looking forward to it more than she had. Perhaps there would be a time in the future when she would be ready to meet a nice gentleman and think about starting a new relationship, but now was not that time.

No sooner had the wave of relief receded than another wave pounded in, this one guilt over possibly messing up her friend's chance to meet someone new.

After all the back slapping was over, she pulled him aside. "I should apologize. If not for me, you could have been matched with someone else. Someone who's enthusiastic to give this a try."

"No way. The grandkids convinced me this would be a good way to get out and socialize." He swept his hand toward her as if doffing his hat for a queen. "Who better to socialize with than you? So you can forget about the apologies," he added with false sternness.

Betty held out her arms as they approached and hugged them both. A group hug, they used to call it when they were kids. "What are the odds of something like this happening? It's amazing."

Henry pushed a hand through his silver hair. "It shouldn't be a surprise. Not only was there a small group for our age bracket, but Mary and I share many mutual interests."

Mary laughed. "Certain portions of our questionnaires must have been identical. I would love to have heard the comments of the Cupid committee members when they paper-clipped our applications together."

Her match-mate pressed his left arm across his abdomen and bent toward her in an old-fashioned bow. "Miss Mary, would you do me the honor of accompanying me on a date to partake in a bit of fun and perhaps a morsel of nourishment?"

She laughed again and dipped into a slight curtsy. "I would be ever most delighted, my dear sir." It certainly wasn't necessary for him to fulfill the date they had agreed to when they signed the registration form. But she was truly charmed that he chose to follow through. "How about tomorrow?

Either before or after our shift at the church booth, we could enjoy the carnival together."

Henry twisted his mouth as if considering the suggestion. Almost reluctantly, he said, "I suppose we could do that. I'll pick you up."

They arranged the time, which was early enough to allow for lunch and a stroll through the carnival games and exhibits before starting their shift. With their date set, he bade her and Betty good night.

"I suppose we should start moseying over to the coat check," said Betty.

It was getting late, and her sister was starting to show fatigue. It would take a lot for Betty to come right out and admit she was running out of steam, so Mary took her hint seriously. "Have you seen Dai—"

Something poked her in the center of her back. Something that felt decidedly like a finger.

"Stick 'em up," said a young woman's voice, followed by a giggle.

Betty looked past Mary and grinned at the perpetrator.

Mary lifted her arms in a gesture of surrender and slowly turned around to find a delighted Chelsea, who held out her arms for a hug. She happily obliged. As they hugged, the baby kicked in protest under the gentle squeeze, setting off a round of laughter between the two. And when Mary explained to Betty and the woman who accompanied Chelsea what had happened, the laughter renewed.

"You and your Cupid date were so cute onstage," the teen said in reference to their corny mugging for the camera. "You seem so perfect for each other, as if you've known each other forever."

Mary hated to burst the girl's illusion that what she'd seen had been a case of romance at first sight. "Actually, we *have* known each other forever. We've been friends since we were children."

"Well, you looked adorable together," Chelsea insisted. She turned and hooked her hand through the arm of the full-figured woman next to her. "This is my grandmother, Patsy Lambert. Grandma, this is Mary Fisher. She's the book club lady I was telling you about. The one I'm learning so much from."

Patsy leaned toward Mary and extended her hand in greeting. Then she shook Betty's hand. The woman wore her dark blonde hair in a chin-length bob. She exuded both sophistication and warmth, a difficult combination for most people.

"I understand we're almost neighbors," Patsy said. She described where she lived, an exclusive neighborhood almost a mile away from Betty and Mary's Shore Drive home. "Now that I know you, I'll make it a point to walk my Jack Russell terrier over there sometime and say hello."

"Please do." Mary's welcome was quite sincere. Chelsea's grandmother seemed very sweet, just like her granddaughter.

Chelsea reached into her pocket and pulled out the program for the Winter Carnival weekend. "Are you going to be here tomorrow?"

She nodded. "A good part of the day."

"Excellent!" Chelsea opened the program to tomorrow's date and thrust it toward her. The blurb announced that

Destiny's Pride, featuring local musician Darius Kerner, would play in the late morning and again in the afternoon. The young man in the head shot wore his dark brown hair in short, rumpled spikes, and he had the slim, angular build of a young man barely out of his teens. "My boyfriend and his band are going to be playing tomorrow. Mostly popular stuff, and some older cover songs because that's what a lot of people around here like. He's really good."

"I'm looking forward to hearing his musical talents." She was also looking forward to checking out the young man who had caught Chelsea's eye.

"There's Aster." Chelsea edged away from the women. "Excuse me a minute. I want to ask her where she got that hot pretzel."

She watched as the girl wound her way through the crowd toward Daisy. Although Chelsea's brunette hair was darker than her grandmother's bottle-assisted blonde, it was easy to see the similarity in their delicate features.

Patsy watched until her granddaughter followed Daisy out of sight, to the pretzel stand. "It's been a pleasure having her stay with me these past few months," she said. "She's a good gal. Very responsible. I think she'll be a good mother."

Mary nodded her head in agreement. "Chelsea has been a real encouragement to the others in the book club. And she's a great help to me in keeping the discussions moving along."

They chatted for a few minutes, and Chelsea returned with Daisy in tow. The younger girl's hands moved enthusiastically as she talked.

"Cute watch," Chelsea said, noting the timepiece on Daisy's arm.

"Thanks. It's an iWatch."

Mary didn't remember her granddaughter receiving such a gadget for Christmas, and to her recollection, Daisy hadn't been wearing a watch at all during the past week. She leaned closer to get a look, but Daisy moved away. "I've never heard of that brand," Mary said. "When did you get it?"

Daisy looked away and waved her hand as if to dismiss the question. "Oh, it's just a techno-gadget."

Betty shifted from foot to foot, which Mary took as a sign that her sister was definitely ready to leave. She was about to wind up the conversation when Chelsea diverted it to Mary's public pairing with Henry.

"Did you see your grandma up there onstage? She's pretty gutsy to try a blind date."

Mary could almost hear the unspoken addendum to the comment: *at her age*.

Daisy abruptly tugged at Mary's sleeve. "Can we leave now?"

No polite excuse for the sudden change of subject. Not a "Nice to meet you" to Patsy. It wasn't like her granddaughter to be so careless with her manners.

Betty gave her a knowing glance, leading her to wonder if she'd come to the same conclusion....

Daisy was embarrassed that her grandmother was going on a date.

The next day, Mary looked up from the table where she shared an early lunch with Henry and watched as Daisy walked a little girl about Ashley's age to a children's game table and helped her pick a string to pull for a prize. Daisy had gotten over her mortification as abruptly as it had appeared, and by the time she had gone to bed, it was as if she had forgotten her grandmother had accepted a date in front of all of Ivy Bay.

From the stage poured a Pink Floyd song extolling the desire for money. Chelsea's boyfriend was actually quite good, and he looked the part of a rock star. Along with the casually spiked hair, he sported a pristine black leather jacket and played a guitar that glistened under the stage lights. Mary found herself tapping her foot to the mesmerizing beat.

"Does Daisy go back home tomorrow?" Henry had to raise his voice to be heard over the music.

"That was the plan, but while repairs were being made on the water pipes at the school, workers discovered asbestos. So she'll be here until next weekend while they finish removing it."

He grinned. "Will she transform back into Daisy at that time?"

"Your guess is as good as mine. I don't know what has gotten into her lately, but I hope this phase passes soon."

Henry waited for her to finish squirting mustard onto her corn dog, then lifted his cola in a salute. "Cheers."

She touched her plastic cup to his. It was so comfortable being with him. She always enjoyed their time together, and she still remembered the weak-kneed relief she'd felt when Katina called his name as her Cupid partner. She'd never been so glad to see him, and she hoped he'd been fully truthful when he said he didn't feel cheated of a love match because of being paired with her.

"To friends," she said.

"To us."

Darius and his band finished the song, and he used the lull between songs to suggest that people to spend their money for a good cause. He reminded them of donation jars at each vendor station and asked everyone to drop some change in them, play some games, and in turn help the people of Ivy Bay who needed health care provided by the clinic. Then he plunked a bucket down at the front of the stage and challenged everyone to fill it up.

Two young girls giggled their way toward the stage and dropped in a handful of coins that clattered a challenge to others to match their donation. Then the besotted girls blew kisses at the lead singer and raced each other back to their table.

Darius thanked the "lovely ladies" sincerely, setting off another round of giggles from the two, and launched into a Bruno Mars song declaring how much he wanted to be a billionaire.

Henry stared down at the cupcake pop in front of him. "I'm glad it was you," he said without looking up.

At first, she thought he was talking about the volunteering she was doing at the clinic. When he still didn't look up, she realized he was talking about their Cupid Couples matchup.

She smiled. "Me too," she said in all honesty.

When they got to the church's information booth a little while later, Dorothy was already there, talking to a young mother. She shot Mary a look that seemed to ask, "Where have you been?" even though she and Henry had shown up ten minutes before their shift was scheduled to begin. Dorothy could be imperious at times, but now she turned back to the sad-looking woman, gave her full attention, and spoke so kindly that Mary couldn't help but be touched.

Mary joined the pair while Henry handed a church brochure to a passerby, and together she and Dorothy listened to the divorced mother of teens describe her struggles. They encouraged her to come to church and let her kids try out the youth group, and they would see what the church could do to help her through her difficult time.

Some people would have ended the encounter with an encouraging hug, but the more formal Dorothy took the woman's hand and held it warmly. True, the prayer group member could use a softer approach at times, but there was no doubt that whenever she put her heart to doing something for the church—for God—she did it to her utmost.

Mary and Henry worked through their two-hour shift, and Daisy caught a ride home with a church member so she could practice playing her flute for a recital coming up later in the school year. When the church-booth volunteers who were supposed to take over at two o'clock had to bow out, she and Henry stayed and filled in for them.

"I don't mind," Mary told Henry. "We would have been hanging around anyway. But if you want to leave, I'm sure I can handle it alone."

"What? And miss seeing you smile at all the passersby? I don't think so." He took off the jacket he had just put on in preparation to leave and laid it over the back of a chair, then settled in for another two hours of answering questions and telling people about the church he loved so much.

At four o'clock, the next pair of volunteers showed up to relieve them, and Mary stretched her back to relieve the kinks.

"It's been a long day of sitting and standing," she said as they prepared to leave for the day.

She was glad their "date" today hadn't been awkward. They'd had a nice lunch, listened to some good music, and laughed their way through the afternoon. All in all, she'd had a good time with Henry, even though most of it had been spent at the church's booth.

"I enjoyed your company today," she told him as they headed out to his car. "Thank you for a nice time."

Henry shook his head and opened the passenger door. "No, you're not getting off that easily. Today's activities were something we would have done together anyway, with or without Cupid's help." He closed the door, then walked around and slid in behind the wheel. "We need to have an official date. A *real* one."

Did he think she felt shortchanged by the unexpected turn of events? "That's sweet of you, but it's really not necessary. We played some carnival games where you spent way too much money for a silly stuffed monkey," she reminded him. "Had a nice lunch. Laughed. If that isn't the definition of a date, what is? Besides, we did way better than those people who meet at a coffee shop for an hour to check each other out."

That, obviously, wasn't what he wanted to hear. "Didn't you read the contract you signed when you registered? We're supposed to go out on a *real* date. This"—he waved a hand toward the park grounds that had temporarily been transformed into a small-town carnival—"was just *hanging out.*"

She didn't recall any such provision but was charmed that he wanted to follow through to the fullest. "It's been so long I'm not sure I remember what a real date is."

"Best I recall, dinner and a movie qualify. How about next Friday? I'll pick you up, and we can catch that comedy everybody's been talking about."

Romantic comedy. Mary didn't know what to think. Was he merely adhering to the Cupid Couples "contract" as he claimed, or had he perhaps wanted something more from their time together? They had been friends for so long it seemed strange to consider going on a bona fide date with him. Strange, but definitely pleasant.

"Friday is good."

He pulled into the driveway and walked her to the door, where he lingered for a long moment while they finished making their plans.

She went inside and watched from the window as he drove away. For some reason, she felt like a giggly teenager about to go out with the captain of the football team.

She let the curtain drop and went to her room to see if she had anything suitable to wear.

TEN

Mary took a seat across from the bank's credit manager, and Henry—her chauffeur du jour—slid into the chair beside her. She hadn't thought to ask him to come in with her, but when he offered, she jumped at the invitation. Considering how much the whole identity theft situation had stressed her, she was glad to have him here for moral support.

After she laid out the situation to the credit manager and handed over her ID as proof that she was who she claimed to be, the woman pulled up the account on her computer and printed out a copy of all activity since the card had been opened.

Mary glanced over the list of charges. The Coach store, Tiffany & Company, and a high-end men's store, to name a few. "Whoever did this certainly has expensive taste."

"If these were truly unauthorized purchases, as you suggest, it may be that someone is using the card to order high-dollar items to resell, perhaps on eBay or Craigslist."

If they were unauthorized? The credit manager seemed friendly and somewhat helpful, but she wasn't saying what Mary wanted to hear. "I didn't make those purchases."

The woman shuffled some papers in front of her. "I hear what you're saying."

Hmm, there definitely seemed to be a note of doubt in her voice.

"Look at me," Mary said, and spread out her arms to display the knit sweater she wore over a plain turtleneck shirt and sensible khaki pants. "Do I look like the kind of person who buys from Coach or Tiffany's?"

Ignoring her question, the credit manager explained the reason for her concern. "The issue is that many of these sales were from the mail-order divisions of those stores." She clicked a few keys on the computer and squinted at the screen. "If they had been shipped to a different address, an automatic red flag would have been raised, especially since it's a new account. But it appears that the orders were sent to your address on Shore Drive."

To her address? Why would anyone do that? This whole crazy situation didn't make sense.

"And then there are charges made to local businesses," the woman continued. "That's a huge question mark for us, because it suggests that you, or someone you gave access to the card, made those purchases."

"Me? You're saying I—"

"I'm just saying that we have to consider all possibilities. I'll turn this over to the fraud department as you've requested. But if it's found that you or your designee made any of these purchases, then all the rest of the purchases—especially those made locally or mailed to your residence—will be suspect as well."

Well, wasn't that a fine turn of events? "This is just so wrong. I came here to discuss the person who had illegally appropriated credit in my name, and now I've become a suspect myself. Where is the justice in that?"

The woman pushed her reading glasses down on her nose and looked over them at Mary. "I understand your frustration."

Mary shook her head. "I'm not sure you do."

"We have to follow procedures. And procedures require that we look first at the owner of the card. Otherwise, everyone would go on spending sprees, then claim to have had their cards or identities stolen."

Mary opened her mouth to protest, but Henry nudged her with his elbow to signal her to give it a rest.

"I'm not saying you did any of those things," the banker continued. "Just cautioning that you may still be on the hook for any charges that took place before you brought this to our attention, or which can't be verified by our fraud investigator."

Elbow nudge or not, she couldn't let that go without a follow-up. "That doesn't make sense. I haven't received any packages from those stores."

Henry leaned forward and rested his arm on the desk. "What can you do to keep this from getting any worse?"

The woman turned back to the computer and entered some information. "I'm making sure there's a hold on the account and will turn the case over to an investigator." She leaned forward and studied the screen. "*Hmm*, there's a note that it had already been frozen, but my records show otherwise." She clicked some keys and turned back to Mary. "No problem. It's taken care of now. Unfortunately, it may take time to sort out how someone came to open an account in your name."

"But I don't have time. You see, I can't continue mooching rides from my friends, and I need to order history books for the sidewalk sale this spring. But that's not going to happen until this blot on my credit history is cleared up so my refinancing can be approved. Do you see where I'm coming from?"

Henry cut her a glance that seemed to say, "Save your breath. It's not going to get you anywhere with this lady."

"I'm sorry for your troubles," the manager said, but her casual tone suggested otherwise—that she was done with the matter and wanted to move on to the next item in her in-box. "We'll be in touch after we have some answers. Until then, I suggest you change all your passwords and make sure your personal identifying information is always locked away in a safe place. Don't give it out unless it's a need-to-know situation."

Disappointed that the case hadn't been solved with a few clicks of the manager's computer keys, Mary thanked her for her time and walked out with Henry to the parking area.

"I wasn't kidding when I said I need that refinancing loan. Worse, if I can't prove I didn't make those purchases and end up getting stuck paying off those ridiculous items, I don't know how I'll be able to fix my car, much less buy a new one." Sure, Betty had already made it clear she'd lend her the money, but Mary didn't want to risk having a debt tarnish their close relationship.

And she didn't want to even consider the absolute worst-case possibility: If the fraud investigator couldn't find the real culprit, the finger of suspicion would be pointed at her. An image of prison jumpsuits popped into her mind, and she wondered inanely if the prevailing prison fashion trend was stripes or solid orange.

Henry touched a hand to her back and gave her a couple of sympathetic pats. He didn't say anything. Didn't have to. It was enough to know that he was there for her in this difficult time, and that he'd try to fix it for her if he possibly could.

Once again, Mary gave thanks for this very special friend.

Mary walked into the health clinic's meeting room a little later than usual to find that the girls had already arranged the chairs in a circle and set out pens for note taking. She would have been here sooner, but she had spent a lot of time calling stores about purchases made with the credit card.

Unfortunately, she didn't get very far. Most could tell her the order was delivered, but they couldn't tell her anything about the person who had placed the order. The Coach store was able to tell her only that a bag had been bought—no surprise there.

Another hour had been spent checking online to see if anyone was offering a lot of NWT—new, with tags—items for sale on Craigslist in the Ivy Bay area after the credit card had been opened. Unfortunately, even if there had been any such ads, they'd already been deleted from the site after a sale had been made.

The girls greeted her as if it had been much longer than a week since their last meeting. They were all talking at once, and it took a moment to sort through what they were saying.

Kaitlyn jumped out of her chair and raised her hand as if she were in school. "My mother saw your name in the paper. If I had known you were trolling for a guy, I could have hooked you up with my uncle Roy. He's really nice."

"Bet he's not as cool as my grandpa," Tamera said. "But he doesn't hear so well anymore, and he refuses to wear a hearing aid. Other than the yelling, he's a lot of fun to hang with."

"I appreciate your caring," Mary said, hoping to forestall further speculation about her love life. "However, I am in no need of any more matchmaking services."

Fortunately, Chelsea and Brianna remained quiet on the subject, but that didn't keep Tamera and Kaitlyn from probing for more information.

Tamera grinned. "So Cupid was good to you, huh? That guy you met, is he cute?"

Mary sighed. If only these girls realized there was more to choosing a partner than the shape of his face or the tone of his muscles. "He has a beautiful spirit."

Kaitlyn pushed back in her chair and stared at her. "A real dog, huh?"

"No, he isn't. I saw him," Chelsea said, breaking her silence on the subject. "He's real nice looking for an—"

Brianna nudged her knee, bringing her friend's words to a screeching halt.

An older man. Mary smiled to let the girl know she was willing to let the comment pass, and Chelsea backpedaled to cover her gaffe.

"He seemed well suited for our Mary."

"Where did you go on your date?" Brianna wanted to know. Her hand fluttered automatically to her collar, silently telling them that even though she had opened up a lot since the group had formed, it was still difficult for her to speak up in front of everyone.

Mary sat down and placed today's reading material on her lap. She may as well answer their questions and get it over with. Otherwise, their book discussion would be constantly sidetracked with questions and innuendos.

"We haven't gone on a date yet. We've made plans to go to dinner and see a movie." To her own surprise, she found she was actually looking forward to it. Her traitorous lips turned upward at the thought.

Tamera reached over and pulled Brianna's hand away from her collar. "What's this? A little something from a new sugar-pie?"

Mary leaned in to see what she was talking about.

Draped around Brianna's slim neck was an exquisite necklace in the shape of an open heart, a dainty pendant Mary had never seen before. As unusual as it was, she was certain she would have remembered it. She glanced at the girl's blush-red cheeks and wondered if it had been given to her by a new love.

"No," Brianna said, pushing Tamera's hand away. "It was a gift." She shyly glanced over at Chelsea, beseeching her friend to rescue her from all the unwanted attention.

Now Kaitlyn jumped into the fray and totally ignored Brianna's answer that the gift hadn't come from a new guy in her life. "You been holding out on us, eh? Was it a Valentine's gift?"

Recalling that the shy girl's boyfriend had dumped her after learning she was pregnant, Mary wondered if they had reconciled. If so, she hoped he would man up and do right by the sweet girl.

"Oh my goodness!" Tamera said, putting a hand over her mouth. "Were you a Cupid couple?" She looked away from Brianna's horrified face and addressed the others in the room. "Can't you imagine the surprise on that guy's face when he first saw our little round friend?"

To their credit, the others refrained from laughing at Tamera's joke.

"No, it's not that," Brianna insisted.

The girl was clearly uncomfortable with the speculations over her private life, and Mary needed to stop the inquisition before feelings got hurt.

"How about *The Valentine Caper*? Did all of you have a chance to read it?" It was season-appropriate; an old mystery, but she thought it held up well over time. Newer books had to be carefully screened to rule out inappropriate language and behavior, and she hadn't had the time to go through new material with a motherly eye. Fortunately, she knew this old favorite would give them lots to talk about without raising eyebrows.

Tamera, however, was like a hungry dog with a meaty bone when it came to Brianna. "Cuz if that necklace came from a Cupid match that you just met, you should give it back, because he's moving *waaay* too fast, girl."

Although Mary agreed, she kept her thoughts to herself and redirected the discussion back to the book. Now, if only she could keep her own thoughts on the book instead of the Valentine caper that had played out with Henry.

Henry pulled into the driveway near where Betty stood talking to their neighbor Sherry Walinski and let Mary out. He waved and pulled away, having promised to give her a ride again tomorrow.

She smiled at the chatting pair and started toward the house, but on noticing their serious expressions, she stopped her beeline to the kitchen to round up dinner. "What's going on?"

"That's what we're trying to figure out," said Betty.

Sherry moved in front of the cat carrier Mary had just set on the ground and made squeaky cat noises to Gus, who ignored her. She rose and filled Mary in on what she'd seen earlier that day.

"That new mail carrier? You know, the one with the surly attitude?"

Nathan Bayard. The man she'd witnessed diverting mail to his shirt pocket.

"Well, I came out to check the weather and see if I needed to wear my medium winter coat or the heavy wool one. There I was, holding my arms out to test how cold the wind was, when all of a sudden, I saw a movement over in your yard."

Sherry stretched out her arm to demonstrate how she tested the temperature against her skin. Using the same arm, she swept it across the front yard to the gate that led to the backyard.

"All I knew at the time was that someone had gone up to the front porch, looked in the window, then strolled around to the back as if he owned the place. You know?"

What business would he have had in their backyard? Something seemed terribly fishy about that man.

"Betty had left to go to the pharmacy a few minutes before that, and Daisy was inside. I could hear her practicing the flute."

An uneasy feeling sank into Mary's stomach.

"He wasn't back there but a minute," Sherry assured her. "If he'd been there even a few seconds longer, I would have called the police. But he's on notice. In this neighborhood, we look out for one another."

"What was he doing in our yard?" Betty prompted.

Sherry shrugged. "I don't know, because I thought it wouldn't be smart to follow him around back."

"No, you did the right thing," Mary said.

"But I did duck around behind the side of my porch and wait until he came back. That's when I saw it was the mailman. The one who acts as though he hates the world."

Indeed he did. Mary recalled the sour expression he'd shot her at the post office last week. "Thank you for letting us know."

Wearing only a heavy sweater over her house clothes on this cold evening, Sherry rubbed her arms, said her good-byes, and scurried back to her house.

"What do you think he was up to?" Betty asked after they'd taken Gus inside and fed him. Flute music drifted to them from upstairs. Since Daisy was preparing for her recital, they decided to leave her to her practice while they prepared dinner.

Mary wasn't sure how, but she supposed Nathan's peculiar behavior could have had something to do with the credit card purchases that had been shipped to their house. She relayed the conversation she'd had with the credit manager earlier that day, being careful to leave nothing out. Then she filled Betty in on the visit to the post office when she'd seen Nathan redirect an envelope to his pocket instead of into the sorting slots with the others. Betty's joints moved slowly these days, but her mind was as sharp as ever, and Mary was hopeful her sister might notice a connection she herself had missed.

"So you're saying you think he may have opened a credit card account in your name and had the packages delivered here?"

"I hadn't wanted to come right out and accuse the man without evidence, but that possibility crossed my mind."

She followed her sister to the sink where Betty rinsed the kale and Mary stripped the leaves off the stems. The stems were too tough to sauté, but she'd save them in the freezer to use the next time she made a green smoothie.

Betty shook water off the kale and splattered Mary's glasses. For some reason—maybe the seriousness of what they'd been discussing, or perhaps because she and Betty needed little excuse to burst into fits of laughter—the droplets all over her glasses incited a riot of giggles from both of them. By the time they could catch their breaths, each was weak from hysteria.

Betty dropped into a chair at the table, and Mary joined her and wiped her glasses with a paper napkin. Every so often, a suppressed snort would escape and threaten to start the silliness all over again.

Once they got their giggles under control, Mary turned back to the subject that had plagued her peace lately. But this time, thanks to the sense of fun she shared with her sister, her heart felt cleared of its former heaviness.

"What I don't understand is, even if Nathan was stealing the packages for himself, why was he prowling around in our backyard?"

Betty shrugged and went back to the stove. "Maybe he's working in cahoots with someone else. Splitting the profits. I suppose he could have left the loot back there for his sidekick to pick up."

Mary rose and crossed to the back door. She flipped on the porch light and stepped outside. No sign of a package anywhere, but she scoured the bushes and behind the lawn furniture anyway, to make sure she hadn't missed it.

Nothing. Nothing left behind. Nothing taken away.

She stepped back inside and locked the door, feeling suddenly very uneasy about the fact that a man had been roaming their private property, especially with Daisy alone in the house at the time.

"We need to ask Daisy if she saw or heard anything today."

As if sensing the unease that had crossed Mary's heart, Betty dropped the spoon into the pot and faced her. "I was only gone twenty minutes," she said. "If I had known…"

"Don't. Don't 'if only' yourself over this." Mary moved closer to her sister and laid a soothing hand on her arm. "Daisy is sixteen years old—old enough to stay by herself for a little while in broad daylight. And you yourself told me that she was perfectly fine when you came back home."

Betty nodded. "If you can call acting like Queen Aster perfectly fine…."

"Well, normal for how Daisy's been acting lately." Mary pondered for a moment, considering something she hadn't thought of before.

"What is it? I can tell by that look in your eyes that you're hatching a plan," Betty said.

"Whoever opened the credit card ordered something new at least every other day. Sometimes more than one order in a day." She retrieved the printout the credit manager had given her and showed the numerous purchases to Betty.

"And?"

"Their access to the card wasn't cut off until this morning, after my visit to the bank. Which means the thief may have placed some orders over the weekend."

"And those orders will be delivered later this week," Betty added, catching her drift.

"Exactly."

"Are you thinking what I'm thinking?"

Mary nodded and tucked the paper back in her purse. "I sure am."

They said the word together. "Stakeout!"

ELEVEN

—◆◆◆—

"Ladies, we've got a lot of praying to do today." Jill Sanderson breezed into the prayer chapel at Grace Church and whipped out a long, narrow list that unrolled like a scroll.

Mary blurted the first thing that came to her mind. "It looks like a naughty-or-nice list."

Jill looked it over as if to verify her comment. "Yes, I suppose there's some of each. But we'll leave it up to God to decide which category the names belong in."

Dorothy, who still exhibited a trace of peevishness toward Mary, crossed the room and thrust a sheet of paper at Jill. At times like this, her manner could seem abrupt or maybe even a bit imperious, but to those who knew her, her brisk style merely meant that she was fully focused on the matter at hand.

"Here are some more names to add that some might say belong in the naughty column, but it's actually quite nice." Dorothy went on to describe her conversation with the mother of teens she'd met at the church's information booth. "This sweet lady has been struggling with her two teenagers who are pitting her and her ex-husband against each other. She's trying to set boundaries for her kids that are balanced between being strict enough for their safety and well-being versus giving them enough freedom."

Heads nodded in agreement. All understood the difficulty and frustration of trying to do what was best for their children while still allowing them to learn and grow.

"I'm pleased to say that she brought her kids to church Sunday, they liked it, and they've agreed to try out the youth group. The mom said she and her family will definitely be back next week."

A hearty round of applause rose from the group of prayer warriors. Success stories like this were part of what kept the ladies meeting week after week, praying for people they knew and for some they didn't.

"Thank you, Dorothy." Jill accepted the slip of paper and added it to her own. "We reached a lot of people at the Winter Carnival. Kudos to Dorothy for suggesting the information booth as an outreach project for Grace Church."

Murmurs of approval echoed through the room.

Dorothy remained standing while she finished saying what was on her mind. "It's always gratifying to do the Lord's work. We volunteers got to spend time with some lovely people we might never have met if we hadn't gone."

Jill made an unsuccessful attempt to stifle a giggle. "And don't forget you and Mary got to spend time with two very nice gentlemen."

Mary's cheeks burned. Now, why did she blush? Going out with Henry was nothing to act silly about.

Dorothy had turned red too, but hers seemed more like frustration than embarrassment. When she addressed the group, her voice dripped with sweetness. "It's interesting, don't you think, that Mary got paired up with our very own Henry Woodrow?" Then, to Mary, "I suppose your connections with your friend, the Cupid committee chairman, came in handy for your matchup."

The others laughed off the comment as if it were a lighthearted joke, but Mary wasn't sure how to reply to such a suggestion. To deny her association with Katina would make her appear guilty of colluding to get a date with Henry, and to acknowledge their relationship—more an acquaintance than friendship, actually—would also make her appear guilty. She and God knew she hadn't rigged the match, so it seemed pointless to debate the matter.

Instead, she changed the subject back to the reason they were meeting this morning. "I could use some prayers," she said, raising her hand like Kaitlyn sometimes did during their book club discussions.

She went on to tell her friends about the credit card debacle. She finished by explaining that this case of identity theft was threatening her chance of getting the refinance loan that would enable her to repair the Impala and order new stock for the bookshop.

"Who do you think did it?" asked Amy Stebble.

It was interesting that the elementary school principal focused on finding the culprit. Mary wished nailing the thief was as easy as making him or her sit in the corner for a short while.

"I don't know for certain, but I'm looking into a few possibilities."

Although she didn't air her suspicions to the group, she found herself rolling them over in her mind once again. Katina had had access to her application that contained all the information needed to open the credit card. And she'd shown her willingness to cross boundaries by, first, rummaging through Jada's purse for a pen, and later, sifting through Betty's and her personal mail. Then there was their temporary mail carrier whose suspicious behavior at the post office, and later in her yard, had raised her eyebrows.

And, of course, there was always the possibility that the guilty party could be a complete stranger. She'd heard of people having their IDs stolen by store clerks, but she hated to think that anyone in her beloved Ivy Bay would do such a thing.

Lynn Teagarden spoke up. "If you haven't already done so, you should change your driver's license so your Social Security number is not on it. They can issue you a DMV number instead."

"Thank you. I'll check into that." It was probably about time to update her license. "Meanwhile, let's also pray for whoever did this. Anyone whose heart told them it was okay to commit this crime needs our prayers as much or more than I do."

"No need to bother with those CDs," Daisy said. "I'll serenade the customers with my flautistry."

Although the word for flute playing had an upper-crust nuance to it, Daisy's use of it lacked the pretentiousness she'd been exhibiting lately. There'd been several occasions at the shop today—now being one of them—when the girl had forgotten to act like her Aster alter ego. Quite frankly, Mary enjoyed the real deal so much better.

By this time, Daisy had been staying with Mary and Betty for nearly two weeks. Repairs to her school's broken water pipe revealed asbestos, which needed to be addressed before students would be allowed to return to class. But today, they learned that school was scheduled to reopen on Monday. Only a few more days to enjoy Daisy's company, and the thought made Mary a little sad. It was times like this when she wished her children and grandchildren lived a little closer. But despite her melancholy over her granddaughter's impending departure, she would endeavor to make the most of their time together and give thanks for precious visits such as this.

Daisy launched into a peppy little tune that showcased her musical ability, but which seemed a little too energetic for the guests who were relaxing in the overstuffed chairs at the back of the shop.

When she came to a stopping point, Mary said, "Do you have something a little more mellow?" The customers at the back were the only two in the store at the moment. They were regulars, and Mary felt certain they wouldn't mind the serenade as long as the music was soft and unobtrusive.

She put the CDs back in the storage box and noticed her favorite Josh Groban CD had developed a scratch, and the Southern bluegrass gospel album had been missing for a while. A shame, too, because although she enjoyed the Heights of Grass, the band had broken up long ago, and she doubted she could find a replacement.

Her granddaughter put the flute down. "Grandma, I'm supposed to learn 'Danny Boy' for the recital, but that's the one piece of sheet music I don't have. Can we go to the music store and see if they have it? I'll pay for it from my allowance money."

"Sure, I suppose so. I could use a new Groban CD too."

Rebecca offered Mary her own car keys and waved the pair toward the door. "I've got it covered."

"Thanks. We'll be back shortly."

Rebecca always came through whenever Mary needed her. She made a mental note to suggest that her employee take time off next Monday to attend Ashley's parent-teacher conference. Come to think of it, perhaps she should give her the rest of that day off as well.

The trip to Ivy Bay's most popular music store wouldn't have been too far to walk on a warmer day, so the drive took only a few minutes. Strings & Things catered primarily to the guitar crowd, but it overflowed with other merchandise to serve all kinds of interests. In addition to musical instruments large and small, there were books and training videos, cleaning and tuning supplies, and of course, the sheet music Daisy had come for. Not only that, bits of whimsy had been arranged throughout the store in the form of windup musical toys and even items to decorate the home, such as coat hooks that looked like small guitar heads.

Over by the wall of stringed instruments, Chelsea's boyfriend demonstrated a ukulele to a twentysomething man in dreadlocks. Mary shouldn't have been surprised to find Darius here. Musicians, especially young ones still struggling to establish themselves in the music entertainment industry, gravitated to day jobs at music stores the way wannabe novelists gravitated to bookstores.

Daisy found the sheet music she came for and loitered in the aisle, delighting in the music-themed decor, toys, stationery, and whatnots that adorned the shelves.

By now, Mary had found the music she wanted, tossed in *The Best of Andrea Bocelli* CD and a collection by the Stutzman Sisters, and took her purchases to the checkout counter where Darius pushed aside a pen and scrap of paper. Finding herself a little short of cash, she pulled out her checkbook to pay for the purchase.

"Go ahead and add my granddaughter's sheet music to the total." It wasn't much, and she enjoyed surprising all her grandchildren with unexpected gifts from time to time. "By the way, it was a pleasure to listen to your music at the Winter Carnival last weekend. I especially liked 'If I Had a Million Dollars.'"

He smiled and looked down at her check as if he weren't sure how to respond to the unexpected compliment. "Thank you. *Uh.* May I see your driver's license?"

She handed him the card, and Daisy called to her from the next aisle. "Grandma, you *must* see this. It's positively adorable."

Ugh. Aster was back. While Darius jotted down the pertinent information on the check she'd just written, Mary turned away and peered over the divider where her granddaughter watched a windup monkey tap a tiny drum while riding a tricycle.

Despite the return of fake-talking Aster, Mary found herself amused at her granddaughter's delight over a simple windup toy. "That's cute, honey. Are you ready to go?"

Daisy waited for the toy to finish winding down, and Mary went back to the checkout to pick up her package. As she did so, she found Darius writing something on the scrap of paper he'd kept by the register.

When he caught her watching him, he hastily pushed the paper aside. Something about his action seemed sneaky, but Mary told herself she was just being hypersensitive about sharing her identification with anyone lately, no matter how legitimate the need.

She accepted the driver's license he returned to her and turned it over in her hand.

To her dismay, there was her Social Security number, printed right on the front.

TWELVE

◆◆◆

Back at the house that evening, Daisy ran ahead with Gus in tow and went inside to help Betty with dinner before the Wednesday night church service.

There had been plenty of work left to handle at the bookshop, but Mary had decided it could wait until next week, after Daisy returned to her home in Chicago. More important this week was the need to spend time with the young woman who, when she wasn't perplexing everyone by posing as Aster the snob, made Mary smile.

Mary lingered at the mailbox, enjoying the crisp February air. Traces of snow remained from last week's precipitation, dotting the yard with scattered small patches of white. One of her customers had called it "seed snow," saying snow remnants such as these grew more snowfalls. Mary loved fall and the slower-paced opportunity it provided for shopkeepers to recover from the hustle and bustle of summer's tourist season, but it was the deeper solitude and solace of winter that reminded year-rounders why it was so great to live here.

The sun had already begun its daily descent, and the cozy town would soon be wrapped in the embrace of dusk. Betty's two-story Federal-style house sat like a haven on the roomy lawn, its light green exterior sending a warm welcome to all those who approached. This was home, and Mary loved every bit of it. But despite the comforting end to a busy day, she couldn't dawdle out here all evening.

She reached into the mailbox and withdrew several envelopes and a couple of advertisements. In an effort to prolong the quiet interlude, she stood at the mailbox and sorted her mail from Betty's. After being inside most of the day, it felt good to soak up the noises, smells, and the flickering sunlight that fell behind barren trees.

Behind her, gravel crunched, and excited little *woofs* broke through her temporary solitude. She turned to see a hyperactive Jack Russell terrier straining and hopping like a child on a pogo stick at one end of a leash and Chelsea clutching tightly at the other.

"Hi, Mary. Pogo, calm down."

Appropriate name. Mary knelt and let the little dynamo sniff her hand. Once his curiosity was satisfied, she rumpled the wirelike hair on his neck and gave his ears a gentle massage.

"What a surprise to see you here," said her unexpected visitor.

"I could say the same about you." Mary rose to her feet and gave Chelsea a warm hug.

The girl seemed a little antsy, perhaps due to the quickly fading daylight. She would need to hurry on her way if she wanted to get home before dark. "Katina suggested I do plenty of walking. She said mild exercise makes for an easier delivery."

"I couldn't agree with her more, but walking at night can be dangerous. Would you like a ride home?"

"No, thank you. Pogo and I will speed it up, won't we, little guy?" The girl turned to go back the way she'd come and glanced over her shoulder.

Mary waved a good-bye and asked God to protect her from drivers who might be tempted to exceed the speed limit on this residential road.

Mary went back to sorting the mail and noticed that the credit card bill had finally arrived. Stuck to the flap was another bill from the same company, that one addressed to Nathan Bayard, the temporary mail carrier who lived a few blocks away.

A weird shiver crept down her spine. Could it be a mere coincidence that Nathan had an account with the same bank? She stood staring at the envelope, wondering what connection this might have with his prowling through their yard recently. She considered sticking the misdirected envelope back into the box, with the flag up for him to pick it up tomorrow. But after recalling the look of surprise on his face after she'd caught him slipping an envelope into his pocket at the post office, and of course his foray into their backyard, she decided to return the bill directly to Nathan—at his house where, hopefully, more clues might reveal themselves.

Inside, after Gus had been fed, Mary pulled the bill for the bogus purchases out of the envelope and studied them.

Daisy whacked a can of croissants on the edge of the counter to make what she called *saucisson en croûte*. Ordinary people called it pigs in a blanket, but that term must have lacked verve according to Aster's way of thinking.

Mary watched her beautiful young granddaughter move comfortably in the kitchen and wondered why she was trying so hard to be someone else. And why especially would she choose to mimic a snooty socialite.

Daisy, please come back to us soon. The thought was as much a prayer as a wish. *We miss the real you.*

At a loss how to handle the teen's strange expression of growing pains, she turned her attention back to the credit card bill.

Just as she had anticipated, several purchases had been made over the weekend, before the bank deactivated the account. The Apple store. And an exclusive department store. Two earlier purchases—from Tiffany & Company— specified on the bill the items that had been ordered: *Elsa Peretti Open Heart* and a code number, but it didn't say what the item actually was. The price, presumably including tax and shipping, came to just over two hundred dollars.

Also listed was a silver chain and pendant. An uneasy feeling settled over her as she recalled the compass pendant Wayne wore on a silver chain around his neck. And what about that pale blue box on his desk? She should have recognized the classic blue color as having come from Tiffany & Company.

Sure, it could be a coincidence. But what if it wasn't?

Daisy put the hot dogs in the oven and set the timer. "Grandma, would you take this out when the buzzer goes off? I need to call Morganna real quick before she sits down for dinner."

"Sure thing, sweetie." She watched as her granddaughter bounced out of the room and wondered if Morganna was the one who had precipitated the change in her. A few carefully phrased questions about the girl were in order before Daisy returned to Chicago this weekend.

Before her mind could follow that trail to its probable conclusion, Betty walked into the room and joined her at the table.

Taking note of the papers scattered across the surface, her sister turned her voice into a whine to parody an unhappy wife. "Honey, you're always bringing work home. We never talk anymore."

Mary playfully swatted her with the lengthy statement, then placed the papers in front of her. "Remember that package you saw on the front porch that mysteriously disappeared?"

Betty nodded as she riffled through the statement.

"According to these charges, there may be more packages coming to the house very soon, if they haven't already been delivered and picked up." Stolen was a more appropriate term, but she tried not to think that way since it only upset her to think of how she'd been used by this criminal. She calculated when the next delivery might be made. "This department store order was made on Friday. And the Apple order was charged on Saturday."

"I was home all day today, and the mailman didn't bring anything to the door."

That simple statement revealed to Mary that her sister had been in pain today. Otherwise, Betty would have walked out to the mailbox to pick up the mail instead of leaving it for her. Even so, Betty had pushed herself to drive over to the bookshop to give her and Daisy a ride home. The sacrifice was duly noted and appreciated.

"My guess is that either of these orders may show up tomorrow. Friday at the latest," Mary said.

"Bob and Rosalba used to deliver our mail in the morning, but the new guy rarely comes before three thirty. He has either turned the route around so he's delivering in reverse, or he's working late into the evening most days."

Given what Dalton had said about Nathan's late start, she guessed he must be delivering into the evening to finish his route each day.

"The book club is meeting at the clinic after lunch tomorrow." The girls had been so involved in their last discussion the group had run out of time to finish, so they'd arranged to squeeze in another meeting tomorrow. "I'll come home right after that. Would you mind lending me your car, or perhaps picking me up at three?"

Betty pushed the bill across the table to her. "Time for a stakeout, huh? Yes, feel free to borrow my car." Her sister flashed her a smile that held no trace of the physical pain she was feeling right now. "What about Daisy?"

"I'll leave her at the shop with Rebecca, then go back and pick her up after I find out what's been going on with these mysterious deliveries."

"Don't think you're going to drop me off while you do your sleuthing," Betty said. "I'm going with you. We're Holmes and Watson, you and I. Maybe Cagney and Lacey." She paused to think it over. "Or is it Scooby Doo and Shaggy?"

Mary frowned. Cold temperatures worsened her sister's rheumatoid arthritis symptoms, and it was possible they could be waiting in an unheated car for quite some time before any activity took place.

"We might end up sitting in a cold car for a long time, with nothing to show for our efforts. I'd hate for our sleuthing to cause your arthritis to flare up."

But Betty was not to be deterred. "I'll bring my hand warmers and electric socks."

Mary thought about it for a moment. "Got an extra pair of those socks for me?"

Her sister grinned. "You've got it, Cagney."

The oven timer buzzed, and Mary pushed herself out of the chair to take out the delicious-smelling hot dog wraps. She carefully arranged them on a pretty blue plate and carried them to Betty.

"May I interest you in a *saucisson en croûte*?"

At the book club the next day, Chelsea wiggled with enthusiasm. "Guess who applied for a job *with* a place to live?"

Since the girl kept darting smiles at Brianna, no guessing was necessary.

Chelsea nudged Brianna with her elbow. "Go ahead. Tell them about it." Too impatient to wait, Chelsea jumped in and told the story herself. "She applied to be a nanny for a one-year-old girl. The best part is, if Bri gets the job, she'll live there full-time. Mrs. Stanley, our nurse? She's so radical. She did some networking and put these two together and, *bammo!* Brianna and this lady are helping each other out." She nudged her friend again. "Tell 'em, Brianna."

Katina had worked fast after Mary had dropped the bug in her ear that the girl needed a job and a place to live, pronto. Mary prayed that, if this was His will, the arrangement would benefit both parties.

"Mrs. Stanley knows a midwife who's friends with the family," Brianna explained. "And she was right. They live in a huge house, almost a mansion. Everything in it is beautiful, and if I get the job, I'll have my own room, and my baby will get its own room too."

Mary noticed that the girl was so excited about this opportunity that she had forgotten to act shy. Silent thanks filled her heart that God had lined up an opportunity that could help this sweet girl out of a difficult family situation. Without this blessing, Brianna could become homeless in a matter of weeks.

"The couple actually likes the idea of my baby eventually becoming a playmate for their child."

Tamera leaned back in her chair and clasped her hands behind her neck. "I can't imagine leaving my kid with a total stranger."

Her tone had been more an observation than an accusation, but Chelsea jumped to her friend's defense. "The parents are going to call Bri's teachers for references. Before Brianna graduated, her teachers always used to rave about how dependable she is, so there should be no problem getting them to put in a good word."

Kaitlyn finally piped in. "That'll be nice. You can sit home and watch TV all day and get paid for it."

"No, it's full-time work. The mom has this cool job where she works from home most of the time. My job would be to keep the kids—hers and mine—entertained and out of her hair so she can conduct conference calls and focus on her work without being interrupted every five minutes. And I would babysit an evening or two a week so she and her husband can go out on dates. In exchange, I would get free room and board, plus some spending money."

Tamera leaned forward. "Get outta here!"

"You go, girl!" Kaitlyn said.

As if suddenly aware she was the center of attention, Brianna smiled and reached for her collar in that nervous gesture of hers. The habit reminded her of how Dorothy often reached to straighten her pearls. But instead of pearls, Brianna toyed with the silver heart necklace that dangled at the hollow of her throat.

"If they hire me, the family will even furnish the baby's room for me. I would feel like a rich girl living there."

Mary recalled Brianna mentioning that she'd never had a room of her own before. Now she and her baby might get their own space. Yes, this would be truly a blessing. She prayed it would work out.

The discussion session ran short today, in part because this was their between-books meeting. To keep from overloading everyone with a full-length novel each time, she had picked out a couple of uplifting articles about new mothers from her stash of *Guideposts* magazines. Just as she had hoped, the brief stories sparked lots of heartfelt discussion.

After their meeting ended, Brianna pulled Mary aside and asked if she'd be willing to provide a personal reference to the couple that was thinking of hiring her. "You're well known and respected in Ivy Bay, and I think your word would help convince them I'm able to handle the job."

The girl had several younger siblings and had mentioned in their discussions that she was no stranger to changing diapers and keeping the little ones safe. Mary hadn't known Brianna long, but she felt comfortable putting in a good word for her.

"Of course, sweetie. I'd be honored to recommend you for the position."

Brianna hugged her appreciatively and followed Tamera and Kaitlyn out, leaving Chelsea to linger.

The pretty brunette hesitated, then handed her an envelope. "If you can come, it would be great, but please don't feel obligated."

Mary opened the pink envelope and pulled out an invitation to a baby shower.

Amity Caldwell invites you to a baby shower for Chelsea Lambert, her best girl friend since kindergarten. Date: Saturday, March 1, at 2:00 p.m. Location: Patsy Lambert's house, 2913 Oyster Shell Drive.

"It's just that I've come to know you over the past few weeks, and you've started to feel like an aunt to me."

Mary returned the invitation to its envelope and tucked it in her purse. The party was to take place a week after this Saturday. She thought ahead, taking inventory of what was on her schedule. Fortunately, that afternoon was open. "I'd love to come."

"There's no need to bring a gift," Chelsea insisted. "Really. You've already done so much for me. Having you there would be gift enough."

Darius showed up and poked his head in the door. "You ready?" Then, seeing Mary, he gave her a polite nod.

Mary waved a hello and reiterated her promise to attend. "I'll be there. Let me know if Amity or Patsy need any help setting up for the shower."

"That's great! I'm looking forward to seeing you then." Chelsea hugged her and dashed out the door with her boyfriend.

Mary picked up her purse and smiled as she pulled the meeting room door closed behind her. She already knew exactly which book she was going to give the baby.

Mary slung her tote full of magazines, Bible, and notepads over her shoulder and headed out past the receptionist's desk where Jada bent over and rifled through a drawer.

"Thank you for booking the meeting room for us," Mary told her.

"Huh? Okay. You're welcome." The pretty young woman looked up from her search, but she seemed distracted, as if not fully aware what they were talking about.

"Is something the matter?"

Jada straightened and placed one hand on her hip. Without bothering to take her eyes off the desk, she said, "I keep candies on my desk for moms suffering with morning sickness, but the jar is empty." She squinted and pushed her hand through the mass of curls that capped her head. "But even my backup stash, which is usually hidden in this drawer, is gone."

"Are you sure? Would you like a fresh pair of eyes to help you look for it?"

"Thank you, but that's not necessary." She closed the drawer with her foot and stared at it. "Butterscotch is Katina's favorite."

A long pause followed.

And then, "Maybe next time I'll get a different flavor." She didn't have to say more.

The nurse-practitioner definitely had issues with boundaries. A thought popped into Mary's mind that she couldn't ignore. Katina had been kind enough to pull strings and get Brianna an interview for a nanny position. All had seemed on the up-and-up with that. But might she have overstepped certain boundaries to do a favor for *Mary*?

"Jada, I'm curious how I happened to get paired with Henry Woodrow for the Cupid Couples matchups." She hesitated, wondering how to ask without sounding unappreciative. "It just seems like an interesting coincidence that he and I were put together. Would someone perhaps have been trying to do us a favor?"

The receptionist quickly squelched that notion. "No, that wouldn't have been possible. We divided the age groups among the committee members who matched their group of applicants. Next, the committee looked them all over together to make sure everyone got a suitable match. Then I compiled the list."

Jada gave Mary a knowing smile.

"Mr. Woodrow must have been quite the catch to have inspired someone to ask to be paired with him."

No names were mentioned, but Mary knew exactly who might have approached someone on the committee for such a favor. Dorothy had been pretty convinced that Henry would be her Cupid match. And when it didn't happen the way she expected, that would explain the steely-eyed expression Dorothy had given her after she and Henry had been paired.

"To keep everything fair," Jada continued, "Katina insisted on an audit of all the matches. Just to be sure no one else had tinkered with the results."

Interesting. This was the impropriety Katina had been accused of. Yet the nurse had been the one to request the audit—quite a different story than the snatch of gossip Mary had heard.

The true version gave her a new respect for the nurse.

THIRTEEN

❖◆❖

Mary slid behind the wheel of Betty's car and a chirp sounded from the passenger seat where she'd tossed her purse. She reached into the bag and pulled out the phone.

A text from Betty: "Lg box just arrived."

She thumbed the keys to tap out a reply: "On my way."

The short drive home seemed much longer than normal, and she fought the urge to speed. Endangering lives was not an acceptable trade-off for catching a criminal.

Betty waited at the end of the driveway for her. Her sister moved quickly to get in the car but fumbled with the seat belt.

Mary reached over to help guide the tab into the slot. "You all in?"

Both thumbs went up. "Hit the gas."

Rather than call attention to themselves by burning rubber, she eased away from the curb and took the first right. Three more rights and the car looped back to Shore Drive. Noticing that Simon Rafferty's car was missing from his driveway, she backed the car in and hoped her blunt-spoken neighbor wouldn't return from whatever outing he was on before the mystery thief had come to claim the box.

"How was circling the block supposed to fool anyone?"

Mary shrugged. "I don't know. It just seemed like the right thing to do."

The car sat at an incline, with the rear slightly higher than the front. Betty scooted down in her seat and reclined the back of the car's passenger seat a little. At five feet three, she hadn't sat very tall to begin with. But scooted down like that, anyone who happened to pass by probably wouldn't notice the fluff of honey-blonde hair that showed over the dashboard.

"If we're going to be here for a while, we might as well get comfortable."

Mary followed suit and slunk down so that the top of her gray curls were the only other evidence that anyone was in the car. She reached into the tote bag and withdrew the Hello Kitty periscope that Ashley had left at the bookshop. Lining up the viewfinder, she scoped out the house and was pleased to see that the yard and large flat box on the front porch were clearly visible. Yes, perfect alignment.

"Did you buy that at an official spy shop?" Betty asked. "I wonder how many FBI agents carry those high-tech gadgets around."

Mary handed over the periscope for Betty to try and pulled her gloves tighter against the chill that had quickly settled over the car. "No need to pay big bucks for the real thing. This shows me all I need to see." In turn, Betty gave her a couple of felt-covered hand warmers in the shape of hearts to slide down into her gloves. "This car could use a seat warmer too. That feature is going on my wish list for my next car."

A white panel truck moved past their line of vision and slowed to a crawl.

Periscope forgotten, Mary and Betty both crept up from their slouched positions.

The vehicle continued past their house, and a squirrel crossed safely to the other side. The panel truck turned at the corner and went on its way.

Mary and Betty slithered back down again. The periscope amused them for a while. Then Mary practiced taking cell phone pictures to see if she could get a good shot without revealing their presence. In hushed tones, Betty filled her in on what was going on with her own book club and the ideas she was considering for this spring's backyard vegetable garden.

"What do you think is in the box?" Betty asked.

The periscope went up again. The viewfinder showed a large flat cardboard box sitting on one end. The brand name Circadia seemed to dance across the surface in a variety of shapes and sizes. "Which store did you say it came from?"

"That department store that's too expensive for us. Lavish Home."

Not too expensive for Betty, but certainly more lavish than Mary's budget could afford. "My first guess is it's some kind of furniture. Maybe a table. Or a headboard. But, considering the type of merchandise that store sells, it could also be a large wall hanging or a mirror."

A car pulled between Mary and her view of the front porch. She ducked down, and Betty whispered, "It's our crook."

Mary pushed the periscope into her sister's lap and inched up in her seat to see the view with her own eyes. An older sport-utility vehicle had parked blatantly in front of their house. The paint job was so weathered from age and harsh Massachusetts winters that it was hard to determine the color.

The door swung open, and whoever was inside spent a moment pulling up the hood on their coat. When he or she emerged, hair color and length, and even facial features were indiscernible. Even the clothing failed to reveal much—unisex jeans, plain black boots, and an insulated hooded coat common to New Englanders.

"Do you see who it is?" Betty asked.

"You're the one with the periscope." They watched while the person strode up to the front door and hefted the cumbersome box. "Walks like a guy."

"Could be a tomboy."

Mary shook her head. "The shoulders are too big to be a female." The ease with which the person carried the box seemed to confirm her suggestion. "Let me see that periscope again."

Mary trained it on the person in hopes of making out a few facial details, but the person turned toward the car to unlock the back, and the box blocked her view. She aimed the scope to get the license plate number, but even if the angle hadn't been wrong, it would have still been unreadable since the person blocked it with his knee.

He shoved the box into the back, slammed the gate shut, and wasted no time getting back into the SUV. He drove away, leaving behind only a plume of exhaust. It was as if neither he nor the package had ever been there.

Betty sat up in her seat and straightened the back. "Wasn't that just as casual as could be? He acted as if he had every right to be waltzing up to our front yard and taking whatever pleased him."

"Where's the key?"

"The what?"

"The key. I need to follow him." A sense of urgency—and the bulky heated inserts in her gloves—had Mary's fingers fumbling over the seat for the errant key ring. Finally, she found them wedged between the seat and the console.

She stuck the key in the ignition but didn't bother to start the car.

"He's long gone," Betty said.

"Yeah. The best we can do now is ask Chief McArthur to keep an eye out for the guy." She pulled up his number on the phone and pressed the Connect button. When he answered, she filled him in on what was going on. "We were hoping you could alert your deputies to be on the lookout for an older-model SUV. The color is dark. Maybe charcoal or faded navy." Or some other color that defied description.

The chief's voice sounded tinny over the weak connection. "Do you realize how many times we come across vehicles of that description every day?"

"Does it help to know that the SUV is rather beat-up?"

"I'll let you know if we see anything." He didn't sound very optimistic.

Mary hung up the phone and had reached to start the car when something pounded against the window beside her. She screamed and flew forward in her seat.

Betty grabbed the plastic periscope and wielded it like a weapon. If Mary's heart hadn't been pounding so hard, she would have found the sight comical.

A dark figure loomed beside the car. The keys had dropped to the floorboard during her startled reaction, so there was no chance of leaving in a squeal of tires on pavement. The person leaned down and shaded his eyes with one hand while he peered into the window.

Simon Rafferty scowled into the car and motioned for her to roll down the window.

Mary's hand flew to her chest, and even through the coat and gloves, she could feel her heart flopping like a dying fish. "Thank goodness! It's only Simon."

She rummaged on the floor mat and once again found the key. This time, she stuck it in the ignition and powered the window down.

"You two park here any longer," he said without preamble, "and I'll have to charge you rent."

———

"Thank goodness it's Friday!" The well-dressed woman of about thirty had come in to trade some books. She opened her coat in deference to the shop's warm interior, pushed a small pile of books across the counter to Mary and handed her the tally card that tracked her trades. "I am so ready to leave the office behind and enjoy the weekend for a change."

Mary had seen her before and assumed she worked in a nearby business office, but something more than her facial features seemed familiar. She looked down at the card in her hand. *Liliana Maclay.*

"Well, feel free to shop while I add these up," she told the woman. "A good book always makes a weekend more enjoyable."

Daisy strolled to the front of the store with Gus in her arms. She looked down at her iWatch in a pointed hint that she was ready to go back to the house now.

"There's no need," Liliana said. "I don't have any time to read lately. Not with a busy two-year-old. I'm just getting rid of stuff I've collected over the years to make room for a play area."

Mary entered the cover prices on the calculator, then multiplied by 25 percent to arrive at the credit owed to the customer. "It's nice to clear out excess items that other people can use. You feel good knowing you've blessed someone else, and at the same time, you're giving yourself some extra space."

"Exactly. I've been on a roll lately. Last month, I finally took my prepregnancy clothes to the thrift shop. After two years, there's not much chance I'll ever fit into those skinny clothes again."

Mary glanced up at the attractive woman before her. If the customer needed to lose weight, she couldn't see it. Although still fairly slim, Liliana had been graced with a few womanly curves, most likely the result of changes the pregnancy had bestowed on her body. "I think you look wonderful."

That's when she noticed what seemed so familiar about the woman. The expensive-looking earth-toned shirt—most likely an exclusive designer top, which seemed perfect for office wear—flaunted a telltale asymmetrical neckline that she'd seen before.

Her gaze automatically went to Daisy. The teen wore an *uh-oh* expression that told Mary something was afoot.

"Gus needs a snack," Daisy announced. She shifted the cat under her arm and bolted for the back of the shop.

At first confused by her granddaughter's reaction, Mary soon realized what had looked so familiar about Liliana. The designer top Daisy wore today—dark orange and a muted blue with a black zipper that zagged across her chest—must have come from that thrift shop. Probably from this very customer. That was the only way she could afford such a pricey item. Understandably, the newly image-conscious Aster would be loath to be caught wearing someone else's cast-off clothes.

But if that explained the sudden appearance of expensive-looking tops, what about the iWatch? Surely such a coveted and trendy gadget couldn't be found in a thrift shop.

She handed the tally slip back to the customer and thanked her for the books. "Come back whenever you get a chance to read again. Meanwhile, enjoy your son now, while he's little."

She glanced over in the direction Daisy had gone.

"They grow up so fast."

"Hang tight. I'll just be a minute." At Daisy's inquisitive glance, Mary added, "I have to drop off this envelope that was delivered to us by mistake."

She pulled up to the address she'd found on the bill and parked in front of the house.

"Couldn't you have just put it in our mailbox with the flag up?"

"*Um*, this is a little more personal." More up close and personal, that is. She scanned the yard to get an impression, to see if anything looked out of place. What she saw, though, was a well-groomed yard around a genteel house that spoke of money. Certainly more than the kind of house you'd see the typical postal employee living in.

She got out of the car and walked across the yard toward the porch. The front door opened, and an über-fashionable woman stepped out.

"Mrs. Bayard?"

The woman pulled her chic scarf around her neck and kept walking to her car. Every hair was in place, her makeup artistically applied, and her clothes the stuff that magazine covers were made of. She looked like a celebrity on her way to a gala. "Yes, but I'll warn you now that if you're selling something, I'm not interested."

Mary changed course and followed her to the car. "You can rest assured, that's not why I'm here." She explained about the letter being erroneously delivered to her and Betty's house and held out the envelope to the woman who peered at it as if it smelled bad.

Mrs. Bayard finally accepted the mail and tucked it into her purse. A Coach purse. A new one, judging by the notable lack of patina on the leather.

"Thank you," she said, and opened the car door. "I'd stay and chat, but I'm on my way to an exclusive function, and I can't be late."

"I understand." What she understood was that Nathan Bayard's wife couldn't be bothered. Mary remembered Dalton's having described her as a high-maintenance wife, and wished she could tell the woman that the true valuables in life were not the things you owned or the people you impressed but the people who loved you. But she couldn't. People had to figure that out for themselves. "You have a nice evening," she said.

The woman flung the purse over her arm, and something dangled from the handle as she moved to get in the car. Although the paper hangtag had been removed, the matching purple string remained attached.

Mary watched, deep in thought, as the woman drove off. There had been a purchase on her credit card from the Coach store. She couldn't say for sure that Mrs. Bayard's bag was the same, but it was one more interesting coincidence.

FOURTEEN

Mary didn't have a fancy purse to carry on her date with Henry, but she felt certain he wouldn't care. Or even notice, for that matter. What she did have, though, was her trusty black skirt that floated prettily around her knees and a three-quarter sleeved, fine-gauge knit sweater in turquoise that she liked to think made her look an inch or two taller.

At the moment, Henry was getting out of the car to come to the house for her, and she didn't want to make him wait. Or, worse, put him through a dating inquisition by her sister and granddaughter.

"You have a good time tonight," Betty said, and straightened the small pendant necklace that had snagged a fiber on her sweater. "Don't worry about us. Daisy and I will be fine."

Her granddaughter gave her the once-over, followed by a nod of approval. "Aunt Betty and I are going to shop from the seed catalog. And then we'll watch *Wheel of Fortune*. Try not to be envious that we're having a better time than you are."

Daisy gave her a quick kiss and a smile.

"Don't believe that," Betty said. "She already has a suspense movie picked out, and we're going to dive into your stash of homemade ice cream."

"*Aw*, why'd you tell her that? Now she's going to wish she stayed home with us."

All the fuss over her date with Henry brought to mind the long-ago time when Betty had helped her prepare for her first date with John. Which wasn't to say she put this date in the same league. All along, she and Henry had been making light of their "official" date, so she wasn't taking it too seriously. In that way, it didn't compare with her first date with John, but it was still a first, in its own way. And her nervousness was showing.

She shrugged her coat on, hugged her family, and slipped out the door before Henry made his way up to the porch.

"Don't forget," Daisy called after her. "Your curfew is midnight!"

Henry grinned and tucked her hand through his elbow. "Did she give you a secret code for calling home if you're not having fun?"

Mary laughed. "No, but she did tell me to text her and let her know how it's going."

The secret code had been an arrangement she had set up with her son Jack many years ago when he had gone out with new friends whose judgment seemed a little questionable, to her way of thinking. Rather than forbid him from going when there was no tangible reason, she told him that if the evening went bad and he felt pressured to go along with anything that made him uncomfortable, he was to call her and say, "I'm calling to check in like you asked me to." That would be her signal that he wanted her to *require* him to come home right away so he wouldn't look like a chicken for backing out of whatever trouble the others were preparing to get into.

Sure enough, less than two hours after he had left, he called and gave her the prearranged message, and Mary had asked, "Do you want me to ask you to come home now?" With an exaggerated tone of reluctance meant for his friends' ears, he said, "Yes, ma'am. If I *haaave* to."

That night, her son had come home with a clear conscience and his "cool" reputation intact. Mary had watched her son take one more step toward manhood that night, and to this day, she still thanked God for guiding him to make the right choice.

Henry closed the car door and slid behind the wheel. "You don't have enough room on your cell phone's text screen for all the fun we're going to have tonight."

He was right about that. Dinner reservations had been made at the Chadwick Inn, a lovely historic inn that attracted a wealthy clientele and offered what Nathan Bayard's wife would have referred to as an "exclusive" menu.

Inside, a waiter laid a napkin across her lap and left them to select their meals from the menu. There was so much beauty in the elegant dining room that she found it hard to keep her attention on the printed offering of scrumptious food.

"I'm a bit overwhelmed," she admitted.

"By the menu? Let me suggest a couple of options I think you'll like."

"Actually, I was talking about your choice of restaurants." She sipped water from the beautifully rounded goblet. "I wasn't expecting you to go all out like this."

Henry inclined his head to one side. "A special restaurant for a special lady. It's only fitting."

Pleased and just a little awkward, Mary fidgeted in her chair. If they were thirty or forty years younger, she might have questioned his motives behind the "special lady" comment, but she knew him well enough to know that if Henry spoke something, it was certainly the truth as he knew it.

An interesting dynamic buzzed between them, and he seemed to sense it too. He raised his glass. "To more than five decades of true friendship."

She clinked her glass against his. "And to many more decades of friendship for the future."

He met her eyes, his gaze sincere. "Yes. I'd like that very much."

Their meals arrived a short while later. Lobster-crusted haddock, green bean almondine, and brown rice quinoa pilaf for Mary. Henry opted for prime rib with rosemary au jus, baked potato, and a seasoned vegetable medley. Absorbed in the delicious flavors and textures that tickled their tongues, they ate in companionable silence.

Silence, except for Mary's moans of delight over the first bite of each dish. After she realized Henry was laughing over her exuberance, she tried to stifle her reactions, but to no avail.

"Me too," Henry said. He dabbed a spot of steak juice at the corner of his mouth and moved to return the napkin to his lap. But with his eyes fixed on her, he misjudged, and the napkin slid toward the floor. In his bid to grab it before it made contact, he bumped Mary's leg with his own. "Excuse me."

Mission accomplished, he held the napkin aloft in a sort of victory salute.

"Nice move," Mary said.

Henry's smile turned serious.

After she'd said the words, she could have kicked herself for making it sound as if she were referring to his accidental leg bump. One minute they'd been relaxed and comfortable in each other's company, and now their interaction had skittered into an awkward weirdness that was unusual for them. To redirect the unspoken conversation that was going on between them, she started telling a story about the first thing that popped into her mind—the stakeout she and Betty had staged. Of course, she didn't come right out and call it a stakeout, but she didn't have to. He knew exactly what she was talking about.

"We were just watching," she said in an attempt to downplay what she and Betty had done. "From across the street," as if that made it any safer. She went on to describe what they'd seen and that they still had no clue who the person might have been. "It would help a lot if we knew whether the guy was working alone or in cahoots with someone else."

Alone? Maybe Nathan Bayard, their temporary mailman. In cahoots? Perhaps Katina Stanley's husband, if he was as worried about their children's tuition costs as Katina seemed to be.

Henry was clearly less interested in the identity of the man who had taken the package than in what that person might have done if he had noticed her and Betty watching from the car. His protective instincts had gone on high alert from the beginning of her story, and now an expression of sincere concern drew a line between his eyebrows.

Gently, as if explaining to a young thrill chaser that jumping off the roof with only a bedsheet for a parachute was a bad idea, he said in all earnestness, "I think you should leave the detective work to law-enforcement officials. That's what they're trained to do. You, on the other hand, are a pro at selling books, and that's what you should stick to."

Instead of taking offense to his admonition to leave detective work to the police, she picked up the real message behind his words. And she felt blessed to know how much he cared. Without considering the implications, she placed her hand on top of his.

"Thank you," she said.

"For what?"

"For caring enough to worry about me."

———

Rather than drive past Boston to Melrose to drop Daisy off with cousins Emma and Luke, they all met in Boston for a couple of hours of shopping and sightseeing followed by lunch.

Mary's daughter was away for the day at a women's church retreat, and her son-in-law Chad brought Emma and Luke to meet them. The plan was for Daisy to sleep over with her cousins tonight, and the family would drive her to the airport tomorrow.

When Mary first discussed the meeting place with Chad, they had originally planned on going to the

Shops at Prudential Center. Daisy, on the other hand, had pleaded to go to the higher-end shopping mall at Copley Place, a few blocks away. Mary and Chad agreed to the teen's request, primarily because they could find a white shirt for Luke's upcoming chorus performance at either place and because the open courtyard in the middle of Copley Place would offer a nice respite from the rigors of shopping.

On their arrival, Mary found herself overwhelmed by all the high-end stores and their spiffy merchandise.

Daisy pressed her nose to the window of a store that offered hip young fashions. A stripe-and-leopard-print dress had caught her eye. "Ooh-ooh, look!"

Twelve-year-old Emma pressed her nose to the glass in imitation of her older cousin. One of Emma's primary pastimes was playing softball, but she was also at that age where she was starting to take notice of fashions. Mary hoped her granddaughter wouldn't be influenced to try this particular style. Better to choose something that reflected her own personality.

Having already bought the white shirt he came for, seven-year-old Luke became bored with the concept of shopping for the sake of shopping. "Let's go play in the courtyard."

"I have a better idea," their dad suggested. "I know this great burger place that's only a few blocks away. It's a real dive, but the food is fantastic."

Mary wondered if it was the same "hole in the wall" place Wayne had suggested when they mentioned going to Boston. If so, the restaurant must be excellent.

Enticed by the prospect of food, they all exited the building onto Huntington Avenue and walked by the Tiffany & Co. jewelry shop.

"Dad, I'll race you to the end of the block," Luke challenged.

Mary held up her hand. "Wait a sec. I want to take a quick peek inside." The credit card statement had shown a fairly recent purchase from Tiffany & Co., and she wondered if she might be able to ferret out some information about the transaction.

"Grandma!" Daisy said. The girl was clearly impressed by her choice of stores for shopping. "Nice taste."

Luke, on the other hand, let his body go limp with boredom and pretended to drag himself to his father's side. "*Puh-leeeeeze.* Save me!"

Chad, a high-energy person himself, seemed to agree with his son's aversion to gawking at decorative objects, though he was too polite to come right out and say so. Instead, he headed over to a cement planter outside the shop. "Tell you what, Mary. We'll wait here, and Luke can show me his latest hacky sack moves."

Excited at the prospect of having something interesting to do, the boy retrieved a colorful footbag from his pocket and began popping it from the top of one foot to the other.

Eager to take their shopping experience to the next level, Daisy and Emma followed Mary into the store, where they wandered and savored the beautiful sights.

"Ooh, Dad would like this," Emma said and then pointed to a silver tiepin shaped like a handlebar moustache.

"That doesn't make sense," Daisy told her. "Why would anyone wear a moustache on their tie?"

"That's what's so funny; it doesn't make sense. But Dad would totally get it."

Well, that made one of them. Mary didn't get the humor either, but what she did get as she leaned over the locked display case of men's jewelry was an eyeful of a small compass dangling from a silver chain.

The piece was an exact match of the one Wayne claimed to have bought on credit because it fit his personality. Mary adjusted her glasses to take a better look at it. Could this have been the necklace and pendant that was listed on the statement? She wished she had thought to bring the paper with her to check it against the inventory number.

The salesperson approached and offered to help them find something.

Mary dragged her gaze away from the miniature compass and reminded herself why she'd come in here in the first place. "Yes, thank you. I'd like to see your Elsa Peretti collection."

"You go, Grandma! You really know your stuff."

If she were the lecturing type, Mary might have pointed out that the jewelry a person wore was always less interesting than the one who wore it. But such instructional methods never went over well with teenagers, so she saved her breath.

Emma bent over the display case. "You would look pretty in any of these, Grandma."

With this quality of craftsmanship, she supposed anyone would look pretty in any of the pieces of wearable art. And the nonwearable decorative pieces would add a touch of whimsy and flair to any home. "Thank you. That's very sweet of you to say."

With so many different items in the collection to choose from, she wished once again that she'd brought the credit card statement with the inventory number on it. So, instead, she perused the display for the right price range and found a lovely silver piece at $195, just under the charge credited to the account.

"Can you tell me how much this would cost after adding taxes and shipping?" Mary felt a little guilty for wasting the lady's time, but traffic in the store was light at the moment, so at least she wasn't keeping her from a paying customer.

The salesperson tallied up the charges and gave her the total; it was the same amount as the charge on the credit card statement. Mary wrote the inventory number on her hand to check it against the credit card statement when she returned home.

The girls wandered off to another display case, determined to take it all in.

"May I wrap this up for you?" the clerk asked.

"No, thank you." According to the statement, she'd already bought the item once, so she certainly didn't need another. "As it turns out, this piece was already ordered to be shipped to my house. I was wondering if you could look up the order to confirm the delivery."

Using the information Mary gave her, the rep looked up the information on her computer. "Yes, it was delivered." To be certain, she read out the address, which matched Mary's.

"Does it mention whether it was an in-store purchase?" If it was, perhaps one of the employees would be able to describe the purchaser to her.

The clerk seemed surprised by the question, but covered her curiosity and looked up the information. "It was an Internet order."

Of course it was. So much easier to remain anonymous that way.

When she and the girls finally emerged from the store, Chad shot a conspiratorial grin at Luke, then turned a mischievous smile on them. "We'll race you girls to the end of the block."

He led the charge, and in the next instant, four pairs of feet pounded down the sidewalk.

Determined not to be left behind, Mary ran too, and surprised herself by making good time despite bringing up the rear. She caught up with her family at the stoplight, breathless and laughing. For the next block, everyone walked while they recovered from the mild exertion, and after the next intersection, Mary initiated the run. The alternating walks and runs provided excellent exercise and helped them work up an appetite until they arrived at the industrial area where the burger place was located.

Still breathing hard from their last sprint, they passed a run-down lot that featured an equally battered building. Not a place that inspired confidence.

Her discomfort must have shown, for Chad hastened to assure her, "This neighborhood is a little older, but it's okay." He laughed and pointed ahead to the Bigger Burger. "The restaurant isn't much to look at either, but we're not here to eat the building."

Luke, apparently unfazed by the vigorous sprints, bounced on his toes. "I could eat it." He pushed out his small belly and rubbed it with gusto.

Her grandson tried so hard to be like his fun-loving dad. She smiled to see the hero worship in his eyes and hoped he'd always try to emulate the good qualities his father possessed.

Inside the restaurant, the noise of the diners echoed against the warehouse-like ceiling. In honor of her visit to Boston, Mary ordered a bean burger, and the girls debated which was healthier: a mushroom burger with provolone cheese or a lobster burger. Luke naturally followed his father's lead and got the works, but only finished half of the enormous burger. They wrapped up the rest and took it with them for him to finish later.

Outside, Luke swung the plastic bag of leftovers over his head, prompting Mary to take it and prevent someone from getting a works burger headache. "Are we going to run back to the mall?" he asked.

To Mary's relief, the family answered in unison. "No!"

Quite a bit slower this time, they made their way past the lot that had given Mary the creeps earlier. The children were debating whether to detour on their drive back to Melrose later to look at the fireboat, when the door of the weathered building burst open and two men emerged.

Angry words ensued, and Mary gave thanks that the children were too far away to hear whatever epithets might have been hurled. A moment later, the men's argument escalated into a scuffle, landing the smaller of the two on the ground. He quickly popped back up, and the larger thug-like man advanced on him, his fists clenched and all the while shouting more angry words.

As if by instinct, Mary started to move the curious children across the street to put more distance between them and the brawl that was about to unfold. And then she saw who the smaller man was.

Honest Wayne.

"That's my car salesman," she said, pointing to the man who lifted an arm to ward off an impending blow.

Chad herded the children closer to Mary and moved toward the fray. "Which one?"

The big guy drew back his fist. This was not going to be a fair fight.

"The one who's about to get beat up!" Concerned for the man's safety, she jumped up and waved her arms, screaming, "Wayne!"

Both men looked in her direction, and Wayne wisely used the momentary distraction to hightail it away from his thick-muscled abuser. His arms pumped and feet pounded as he rounded the corner of the building and headed down a narrow alley.

The goon, in hot pursuit, took off after Wayne, and Mary dreaded to think what might happen if the guy caught up with him.

As if one man wasn't enough to worry about, Chad sprinted across the street and followed the pair down the alley, out of sight.

"Get 'im, Dad!" Luke hollered. He tugged at Mary's hand. "Let's go watch."

Before Mary could react, the girls grabbed the boy by both arms to keep him from following his father.

For added insurance, Mary grasped the back of her grandson's jacket and held on tight. With her other hand, she reached into her purse and pulled out her trusty phone. One-handed, because she wasn't about to let go of Luke for him to join the trouble, she dialed the emergency number.

Quickly, she reported their location and explained the situation. "I'm worried about my son-in-law. He went after them to help. Please send someone quickly."

Just after she hung up, a lone figure emerged from the alley beyond the decrepit building.

"Chad!" Mary stopped the children until a car passed. Then they raced toward him at an even faster pace than when they had sprinted to the burger restaurant earlier. All five of them embraced in a tangled hug that threatened to squeeze the air out of the would-be rescuer. After a moment, she stepped back and took a hard look at her son-in-law who was still breathing hard from his run. "Are you all right? What happened?"

He shook his head. "I lost them."

Daisy pulled away from her uncle, a look of concern marring her pretty features. "Do you think that mean guy got the smaller man?"

Chad paused for a moment, as if considering whether to shelter her from the painful truth, then apparently decided against it. "I don't know," he said. "The last I saw of them, the big guy was moving pretty fast."

Mary groaned to think what might have happened after the pair had passed out of Chad's view. Wayne was a nice enough guy. Always smiling. Unfortunately, his smile didn't seem to be of any help against his attacker.

Chad put his arm around Mary's shoulder. "We did all we could do."

"My dad's a hero," Emma said, as if suddenly realizing the magnitude of what had just transpired.

Indeed, he was. He had bravely followed the two brawling men into an isolated alley, prepared to defend Wayne as much as humanly possible. Now the rest was up to God.

Mary thanked God for protecting her big-hearted son-in-law and prayed that her distraction had given Wayne enough of a head start to escape.

FIFTEEN

◆◆◆

After yesterday's excitement, Mary was glad for the opportunity to spend a quiet time of reflection at Grace Church, with Pastor Miles continuing his series on the enduring power of love. Her soul always felt either soothed or stirred after one of his sermons, and today she was glad for the comforting message in his words.

After the closing prayer, she followed Betty to the exit where Pastor Miles and his wife, Tricia, shook hands with the departing parishioners. When it was their turn, Betty took their hands in both of hers. "Thank you for a lovely sermon today. Considering the light that shines between you two, you definitely know whereof you speak."

Mary nodded in agreement. The happily married couple knew the meaning of love, which overflowed from them to all they encountered, including their eight-year-old autistic grandson, whom they adored.

"How did your date with Henry go?" Tricia asked.

With people lining up behind them, Mary kept it short. She briefly described the luscious dinner at the Chadwick Inn and the silly but enjoyable humor in the movie.

Behind her, Lynn Teagarden said, "Dinner and a movie, huh? That's quite the cliché."

Her comment prompted others to weigh in on whether it had been an acceptable date or not. Some implied that because it was a traditional choice, it must have been boring.

Apparently realizing what she had unleashed with her innocent question, Tricia quickly added, "There can't be a boring date unless the people themselves are boring. And you two are anything but." She squeezed Mary's hand. "I'm glad you had a good time."

Tricia was right. Their date had been anything but boring. "It helps that Henry is such a good conversationalist," she confirmed. "He seems to know a bit about everything."

Someone moved past them in the small foyer to leave the cluster of people that clogged the exit.

Mary distinctly heard a *"Harrumph"* as Dorothy scooted past them.

———

The next morning, Mary was standing in line again, this time at the post office to mail a book to a customer along with a couple of payment envelopes.

Hurry up and wait. Her toe tapped the floor with an impatient desire to be on her way. As soon as she realized what she was doing, she stopped herself and tried to tamp down the sense of urgency that urged her to hurry and do what? Nothing that couldn't wait. Sure, there was plenty of work to be done at the shop. But there was *always* plenty of work waiting for her.

Experience the moment, she told herself. *Just be.*

To distract herself, she tried striking up a conversation with the customer in line behind her, but the woman wasn't very receptive. Probably in a hurry to be on her way, Mary thought. She should pause and enjoy the little moments.

Mary turned her attention to the racks of envelopes, boxes, tape, and greeting cards for sale. The colorfully decorated padded envelopes especially appealed to her. Next time she mailed a gift to one of her grandchildren, she would use one of the balloon-printed envelopes for an extra-festive touch.

Her focus moved to the street map of Ivy Bay that covered a large section of the wall. Neighborhoods were divided into grids showing the zip plus-four zones. Studying them, Mary mused over how efficient such a method had come to be. Some people complained about the quality of the postal service, but until recently—when Nathan Bayard had temporarily taken over their route—she'd had no problems. She adjusted her glasses and searched the map for her street and its corresponding plus-four designation.

The queue moved forward, and Dalton motioned her to the counter. He didn't have time to chat today, so while he weighed and stickered her package, she watched the behind-the-scenes activity that once again featured Nathan at the sorting bins. And once again, an envelope got diverted to his shirt pocket.

"Anything else?" Dalton asked.

"A book of stamps, please. I'm one of those dinosaurs who still pays some of her bills the old-fashioned way." Unfortunately, the same could not be said for her alter ego who had electronically impersonated her to open the credit card account in her name.

He handed her the stamps and a receipt.

Forever stamps. As far as she was concerned, only God could give her something that lasted forever, but she was glad these would still be good for use after the price inevitably went up again. She tucked them in her purse, wished Dalton a good day, and headed back outside.

On the other side of the open chain-link fence that separated customer parking from the employees' entrance, Nathan rolled a mostly filled cart to his delivery vehicle.

Mary waved and called out to him. No time like the present to ask a few pointed questions.

He scowled and acted as though he didn't have time to be bothered.

Determined to get some answers, she called to him again and waved a hand as if she were flagging down a taxi. "Excuse me! May I speak to you for just a moment?"

He stopped what he was doing and sighed in a way that made him appear to physically deflate, then walked over to her. "You want something?"

The message was clear: *Make it quick. I don't have time to waste on you.*

Her gaze went to the envelope in his pocket and landed on a dark spot on his shirt. "Yes, I'm Mary Fisher. My sister and I live on Shore Drive." She gave him the street number, and he nodded as if she were boring him. "I wanted to tell you that an envelope addressed to you was accidentally delivered to me the other day. So I dropped it off at your house."

"Yeah? You could have just stuck it back in the box, and I would have picked it up the next day."

That again. The solution that kept popping up after the fact. "I was just being neighborly. And I only mention it now because I wanted to make sure you knew about it." Because she hadn't delivered it directly to his hand, it could still be in his wife's shiny new purse.

Her gaze dropped to his shirt again. What *was* that on his pocket? At an arm's length away, the dark spot hovered at that difficult distance for her bifocals—too close to see through the top portion and too far away for the reading section.

"Yeah, okay," he said. There was no "thank you" or "kiss my foot."

"Excuse me, but you have something on your shirt. Right there." She reached out and moved the envelope for him to see, and in doing so, she noticed the piece of mail was addressed to N. S. Bayard.

He looked down to where she pointed. "It's ink. The postmistress ran out of pocket protectors when they hired me," he said, his voice dripping with sarcasm. "Is there anything else?"

Not bothering to wait for her response, he turned to leave.

"As a matter of fact, there is." She crossed her arms over her chest, then quickly uncrossed them so as not to come across as adversarial.

He turned back to her, his efforts forced as if he would rather be elsewhere, and circled his hand, encouraging her to make it snappy.

"I'd like to know what you were doing in my backyard last week."

He paused and granted her a long-suffering frown, then lifted his hands to form finger quotes. "My job."

"The last time I checked, our mailbox was located at the *front* of the house." She tried not to let his negative attitude affect her, but she was starting to get fed up with his rudeness.

"Look, I delivered a package that was too large for the mailbox. I saw somebody moving around in the back and took it there to deliver it in person. Extra-special delivery, you know?"

Her skepticism must have shown. Nathan Bayard, who acted as though his postal carrier position was beneath his abilities, going the extra step for customer service?

But what if he was telling the truth? Could it have been Daisy he saw? Or was he lying?

"By the time I got back there," he continued, "whoever it was had gone. So I left the package on a chair on the back deck."

He seemed to challenge her to refute his story.

Mary frowned, trying to recall the events as they had unfolded that day. "I don't remember seeing any packages on the back deck."

Unconcerned, Nathan shrugged and walked away.

"Pussycat, pussycat, what have you there?" Ashley asked in a chirpy singsong. "Did you find something under that chair?"

Gus's gray-furred rump pointed skyward, and his tail flicked with interest while he batted at something under the stuffed chair at the back of the shop. In warmer months,

Mary had rescued a cricket from him that had managed to find its way inside and hide from human eyes. But the end of February was too cold for crawling creatures to be lurking about. Maybe a leaf or twig had been tracked in on someone's shoe.

Then again, considering his all-consuming interest, it could possibly be a forgotten bit of a kitty treat.

Without fear or squeamishness, Ashley reached for the thing Gus was playing with and pulled it out.

Gus naturally assumed she had done so to give him easier access to the found object and tried to pull it from her hand.

The scene was too cute for words, and Mary laughed at the interaction between the two.

To move out of his reach and keep him from trying that again, Ashley stood and pressed a button on the square-faced electronic device she'd retrieved from under the chair. "This is interesting."

Mary stepped closer. "Oh, it's Daisy's iWatch. She must have taken it off, or maybe it slipped off her arm while she worked on her term paper in that chair."

Gus yawned, showing his boredom at the derailed game. With an annoyed flip of his tail, he sashayed away between the bookshelves to find another source of amusement.

"Actually, there's no such thing as a true iWatch." The young girl spoke with respect, taking care not to act like a know-it-all. If anything, she seemed apologetic for correcting Mary's misperception. "The company probably isn't interested in making watches that do everything because most people have all they need on their iPhones."

"Really?" She was certain Daisy had called it an iWatch. And she was amazed how kids as young as Ashley could keep up with the ever-changing trends. "Then what would this be?"

Ashley slid the watch face off the mesh band. "It's an iPod Nano—one of the smaller, older versions—and she clipped it on a regular fabric band." The girl fidgeted with it and showed her the separated parts. "Like this. See?"

Mary remembered when Daisy had received the miniature iPod for Christmas barely more than two years ago. Two years, and now it was considered outdated technology.

Her little friend tapped a button to "wake it up," and an analog watch face showed up on the display screen. "Oh, cool. She set it to default to a watch face instead of the main menu." Ashley laid a finger against her cheek while she considered how Daisy had MacGyvered the gadget. "That was quite clever of her. A do-it-yourself iWatch. She probably found a demo video on YouTube that showed her how to do it."

Now Mary understood. The iWatch must have been an attempt to try to impress others with what appeared to be the latest and greatest techno-gadgetry. She held out her hand for Ashley to give it to her.

"Are you going to wear it?"

Mary shook her head, as much in response to Ashley's question as to her dismay over Daisy's apparent need to fit in and impress people. "No, I'm going to give it to Daisy the next time I see her."

"You mean Aster?"

"No, I mean Daisy." She would also try to give her granddaughter some perspective on what it meant to be a child of God. She wanted her granddaughter to know that no fancy iWatch, designer clothes, or other pretense are necessary when you're clothed in God's glory.

———

A number flashed on the electronic screen over teller number three at the Department of Motor Vehicles, and a bearded man in a hunting jacket made his way to the counter.

Mary checked the number on her ticket. At this rate, she'd be here for a while. The wait would be worth it, though, if removing the Social Security number from her driver's license prevented anyone else from stealing her personal information.

Nearby, a toddler in denim overalls pushed his own stroller between the rows of seats where patrons waited for their numbers to be called. His mother seemed not to notice his collision-filled exploits against people's shins as she carried on a louder-than-necessary conversation on her cell phone.

From the corner of her eye, Mary noticed a man hobbling up the aisle on crutches. Her actions automatic from years of practice, she put her hand out to prevent the stroller from scoring a direct hit on the man's leg.

"Hold on a minute." The child's mother flashed Mary a dirty look and called the child over to her.

"Good reflexes," the man said. "Thanks for sparing me further pain."

Mary looked up to see a smiling Wayne Chapman propped clumsily against a pair of crutches. A rigid brace had been affixed with Velcro over the top of his left pants leg, and despite the ever-present smile, he appeared distracted by his injury.

"Oh my goodness!" She stood so he wouldn't have to bend over to talk to her. "Are you all right?"

A sheepish grimace crept across his cheerful face. "It's just a minor break of the kneecap. I'll be okay in a few weeks."

"How did—" Mary cut herself off. She knew the answer without asking, and she really didn't want to hear the gory details of the damage that horrible thug had inflicted on this sweet, mild-mannered man.

"It was really quite silly. Saturday night, after I went to bed, I had a bad case of jimmy legs. With all the twitching and jumping going on, I fell out of bed onto the hardwood floor. Landed smack-dab on the knee." He forced a laugh. "Guess I need to put a padded rug next to the bed in case of a future tumble."

The claim sounded preposterous, especially since he knew she'd seen his altercation on Saturday, but who was she to challenge his story? Still, she couldn't help wondering how long it took that goon to catch up with him in the alley. And considering the damage that guy had apparently done to Wayne, she gave thanks that Chad had not also been caught in the thick of their disagreement.

"Thank you for looking out for me," he said.

Mary nodded, unsure whether he was referring to her distracting the big guy on Saturday, or preventing the child from jamming the stroller into Wayne's leg. He didn't seem to want to bring up the incident near the burger place, so the subject hung in the air between them like mozzarella cheese dangling from a pizza eater's chin, and neither wanted to mention it.

He rattled the folder of papers clutched in his hand. "Guess I'd better take care of the paperwork for the latest shipment of cars. By the way, I'm sorry to say the Impala that I was checking out for you fell through."

"Not a problem," Mary said with utmost sincerity. "Please don't worry about searching for another. It looks like I'll be keeping my car after all." At this point, the odds of getting the loan refinanced were not looking good.

To his credit, he didn't try to push her to buy a new car. "I understand. We'll get your Impala all fixed up for you." With that, he wished her a good day and hobbled off.

She watched him limp away. Broken kneecap. In a flash, she recalled his favorite reading material—Las Vegas mysteries set in casinos—and remembered the thought she'd had about selling cars being a gamble.

Chief McArthur had mentioned an illegal gambling ring in Boston. Could that scuzzy-looking building have been where people like Wayne went to get some backroom gambling action?

Her stomach knotted with tension as she considered the possibilities. That thug. An enforcer for a loan shark? And if so, how much was Wayne in for? If the sum rated a broken kneecap, it must have been a lot.

She watched as Wayne made his way to the counter and placed a pile of paperwork in front of the teller. She had filled out a ream of paperwork in his office a little over a month ago: A preapproved loan application to buy a car in case she found one she liked. All the info she had blithely handed over to him that day could have been used to open a credit card account in her name. The bank's credit manager had suggested that someone could have been ordering all those high-dollar items to sell on the Internet. If Wayne had set up this scam, had he intended to use the money from selling the merchandise to pay off his gambling debts?

It all seemed pretty far-fetched, but it made sense. The pieces, like a puzzle, fell into place.

Mary's number flashed over teller number two. She took her place at the counter and tried not to smile for her picture, as the teller had instructed. Perhaps the request for a serious face was so the image would match the driver's *I'm in trouble now* expression if he or she ever got pulled over. However, it went against her nature to stare expressionlessly into a camera lens.

A few minutes later, she walked away with a new driver's license, complete with a photo that made her look more like Marty Feldman than Mary Fisher.

She and Wayne crossed paths again on the way out, and she remembered the prescription receipt he'd left in the book he'd traded in. She told him about it and added, "It's in an envelope behind the counter. Just ask Rebecca or me for it next time you're in the shop."

Wayne lifted a hand to wave away the suggestion and nearly lost his balance on the crutches. "Just toss it," he said. "The medicine's not working anyway."

"Sure, but the next time you're in the area, stop by the bookstore. We just got the next book in the series you're reading. *Winner Takes All.*"

He continued his laborious trek toward the door. "Thanks, but I'm taking a break from reading those books for now." The electric doors slid open, and she watched as he made his way through. She didn't blame him for putting the gambling mysteries on hold for a while. The stories might be hitting a little too close to home.

SIXTEEN

◆◆◆

On her way back to the bookshop, Mary stopped at the pharmacy, purportedly to pick up butterscotch candies to replenish the clinic receptionist's supply, but there was another underlying reason.

The next aisle over, Chief McArthur browsed the selection of chewing gum options. He seemed lost in thought over whether to choose the blue package or the green, so she continued on her way to the next aisle to the hard candies.

The conversation with Wayne still fresh on her mind, she took the candy to the pharmacy in the back to check out. While there, she got to the other reason for stopping in.

"I was wondering if I could get a copy of a pharmaceutical handout for a particular medicine."

"Certainly." Pharmacist Jacob Ames printed off two pages of information and handed it to her. "Let me know if you have any questions."

"Thank you."

Mary stared down at the paper in her hand. Ropinirole. The medication's primary use was for Parkinson's disease. She edged closer to the eye drops display to leave room for other customers to move past and tried to remember if she'd seen any signs of the condition in the car salesman. She didn't recall seeing the classic tremors in the affable man, and his motor movements had seemed fine when he took off running down the alley. Most of all, his thinking seemed clear and logical. Sure, he'd almost lost his balance when she was talking to him at the DMV a little while ago, but that could have been due to his inexperience on crutches.

She said a quick, silent prayer asking God to heal whatever was ailing the salesman and was about to continue her reading when her cell phone beeped a soft alarm to remind her the book club would be starting before long. Today, they would talk about Sue Monk Kidd's *The Secret Life of Bees* and discuss the qualities that make people a family, regardless of their genetics.

She tucked the handout in her purse to finish reading it later, when she had more time to study the fact sheet. On her way out, she noticed the headline on a stack of *Ivy Bay Bugle* newspapers in a display bin near the exit. "Gamblers Aced: Ivy Bay Parlays Aid to Boston to Flush Out Gambling Ring."

Curious, she picked up the newspaper and scanned the front page. Wayne's name didn't appear anywhere in the article, but the author apparently had a good time lacing gambling terms throughout the piece. A small head shot of Chief McArthur accompanied the article, and the caption explained that Ivy Bay's role in the sting came about after it was suspected the gambling money was being laundered through a local business.

Mary scanned the store and found that the chief had decided on the gum and added a small notepad to his purchase and was moving to the cash register at the front of the building. She got in line behind him with the newspaper.

"Congratulations on a job well done," she said. "Nice photo too. It almost makes you look like Matt Dillon on that old TV show *Gunsmoke*."

He laughed. "I suppose my mother would approve."

It wasn't clear whether he was referring to the job well done or the photo, but either way, she was sure all his loved ones were very proud of him. "You must be pleased at having helped round up those criminals."

"Pleased to finally get some rest," he admitted. "We've been putting in a lot of hours up until Friday when the bust was made."

Friday? That was the day before she came across Wayne being threatened and chased by that big guy. If the bust had happened the day before, what was Wayne doing there in Boston on Saturday? And why had he been chased down the alley where she presumed his kneecap had been broken?

The chief moved to the counter and paid for his gum and notepad, then stepped out of the line to make room for Mary.

She paid for the newspaper, then rejoined him to continue the conversation. On a hunch, she asked, "Would the bust, by any chance, have taken place on Packie Street, near Huntington Avenue?" At his frown of contemplation, she added, "Next door to the Bigger Burger?"

He smiled. "That place has great burgers. The 'cardiac delight'—bacon, cheese, and sausage—is the best. But, no, the place you're talking about is supposedly a fly-by-night used-car dealership. I wouldn't buy from there if I were you."

His face clouded over, suggesting he knew something he wasn't telling her.

She stuffed the newspaper in the bag with the candy and walked with him to the door. "Like it or not, it looks like I'll be hanging on to the Impala for a while longer. So I won't be shopping with them, but thanks for the warning."

"Good," he said, and held the door open for her. "My aunt had an Impala, and it held up pretty well."

Outside, a cool breeze teased at the scarf around her neck. She and the chief were about to go their separate ways when she decided to mention what had been on her heart since witnessing the drama on Saturday. Concern for Wayne overrode her resistance to sharing what could be perceived as gossip.

"I asked about that place because I saw something quite disturbing happen there over the weekend." She went on to describe the frightening encounter and the car salesman's subsequent broken kneecap.

Chief McArthur put on his hat against the sturdy breeze. "I'll look into it," he promised.

"Thank you," she said. "I hope it was just a little spat and that his injury is merely a weird coincidence."

And, even though Wayne hadn't been implicated in the gambling ring, she hoped he wasn't into something equally shady in the car business.

On the Saturday of the baby shower, a pretty young lady welcomed Mary into Patsy Lambert's house. "Hi, I'm Amity. If you're here for baby fun, this is the place."

Mary followed Chelsea's self-proclaimed bestie into the tastefully decorated home that already overflowed with well-wishers. There was Patsy, of course, who flitted from kitchen to serving table, refilling punch and noshes. The girls from the book club. And, of course, assorted neighbors and family members. Across the room, Mary noticed an attractive couple whose dark hair and stunning eyes reminded her of Chelsea's.

She laid her gifts beside the others on a pink decorated table: *Good Dog, Carl,* her favorite first book for children, and a sounds-of-nature machine to soothe the little one to sleep at night.

Next, she sought out the couple she'd seen from across the room. "You must be Chelsea's parents."

The pair glanced furtively at each other before confirming the fact. They seemed nice enough but were very stiff and seemed not to be making much effort to participate in the festivities. Everyone else, on the other hand, seemed to be having a great time enjoying the food and talking about babies. To be gracious, Mary chalked up their standoffish behavior to the fact that they were probably still tired after their drive from Quincy this morning.

After a few unsuccessful strained attempts on her part to engage the Lamberts in conversation, Mary excused herself and sought out Amity to offer a hand wherever help might be needed.

At that moment, the guest of honor made her way over and offered a warm hug. "I see you've already met Amity. We go a long way back."

"Since kindergarten," Mary said, recalling the claim to fame that had been printed on the invitation.

"Yep, she's the bestest. Let me show you the nursery."

A number of the guests followed Chelsea to the small room off the hall. Pogo the dog trailed everyone in and bounced to get his mistress's attention, but she was focused on other things at the moment.

Mary took in the cozy little room while Chelsea went around displaying the collection of cute newborn clothes and other necessities that had already been bought or gifted.

The mom-to-be walked them past the new crib that Darius had brought over and set up. A Mac laptop sat on a small changing table, its screen facing toward the crib.

"Are you planning on raising the next IT genius?" one of the guests asked in reference to the computer.

"No, the laptop is going to serve as a baby monitor so I can watch and listen from another room. It seemed silly to put the money into a dedicated device when a computer serves lots of other purposes as well."

Mary continued wandering through the beautifully decorated room, admiring the pretty setup for the baby whom she was sure would be loved very much. The precious baby items brought to mind the anticipation over the arrivals of her own two children, and later over the arrivals of her three grandchildren. A silver spoon sat beside a tiny porcelain bowl on the night table, all in readiness for the child's first solid foods. The handle of the spoon was designed with an open heart that would serve equally well for hanging on a hook or gripping during those messy feedings.

Her attention went back to Chelsea who was wrapping up the tour of the baby's room. Despite her apparent joy over the little one's imminent arrival, an underlying sadness permeated Chelsea's disposition.

A glance around the room revealed the absence of one key person. Though it was common for fathers to attend baby showers these days, Darius was nowhere to be seen. Mary recalled Chelsea mentioning during their book group that her boyfriend had been distant since learning of the pregnancy, and the girl had worried that he would take off like the father of Brianna's baby had done.

Mary hoped there was nothing to her concerns, but it didn't look good that he lived right on this block and still hadn't managed to pop over to say hello and be a part of the fun.

A motion to her left interrupted her thoughts. Pogo, apparently bored with the lack of activity despite all the people clustered in the room, grabbed a scrap of brown shipping paper out of the daisy-covered wastebasket and tried to initiate a game of chase.

Chelsea put a hand to her forehead in a gesture of annoyance that indicated she was all too familiar with this kind of behavior. "Would somebody grab that from him? He has a terrible habit of eating paper and barfing it up later."

As the closest one to the little masticator, Mary reached for the paper, but the furry little bundle of energy decided to turn it into a game of keep-away. Chelsea's young cousin, a girl of about ten, squealed with delight and grabbed at the dog, which then zoomed by Mary's outstretched hands.

With a speed that Mary didn't know she possessed, she lunged toward the sassy little dog and snatched the paper before he could choke on it.

A ripping sound told her she had been almost quick enough. She stared down at the remnant of the paper in her hand. All that existed was a portion of the address label with the nine-digit zip code on it. Meanwhile, Pogo made gagging sounds as he choked down the portion Mary hadn't rescued.

After the wad had gone down the hatch, he hacked once and gazed up at her, his mouth open in a pant that looked like a ridiculous smile of victory.

Outside, a rattletrap car pulled up in front of the house. The excitement with the dog now over, Amity went to the window and pulled the curtain aside. "Look who's here!"

Mary and the others strained to see the visitor who emerged from the dusty brown SUV.

As he turned toward the house, Chelsea visibly appeared to melt with relief.

Although his car wasn't much to look at, Darius looked spiffy in the new leather jacket he'd worn to perform at the Winter Carnival. He stopped, turned back to the car, and retrieved a large bouquet of flowers from the seat.

A mischievous grin on her face, Amity raised her hand to get everyone's attention. "Let's go in the other room and overwhelm him with all these women."

Before she knew it, Mary got caught up in the surge of bodies moving toward the door as one. She stuck the wrapping paper in her pocket to throw away later and followed them into the living room.

Just as Amity predicted, the dad-to-be reacted with amazement and was overwhelmed at all the friendly greetings and congratulations the women threw at him. Although he'd been perfectly at ease singing in front of a large group of strangers at the Winter Carnival, today he reacted to the crowd with an awkward shyness.

He stood inside the door for a moment, as if deciding what to do next. Finally, he smiled and motioned Chelsea to come to him. When she did, he gave her the flowers, and a chorus of aws went around the room.

Chelsea took the flowers and moved to kiss him for the unexpected gift.

Darius, however, seemed so focused on what he was doing that he didn't notice. Instead, he dropped to one knee and took her hand in his.

The physical reactions of the women who watched ranged from hands over hearts, to hands covering mouths open in awe, to tissues dabbing at eyes. Mary's reaction was to offer a silent prayer for the little family.

Amity took the flowers from Chelsea and stepped back while everyone waited for what was next to come.

However, instead of going straight to the proposal, Darius launched into an apology. "I'm sorry I'm late for the shower," he said, gesturing toward the bouquet in Amity's hands. "I went to pick up flowers."

Chelsea smiled down at him and squeezed his hand in both of hers. "That was sweet."

"The flowers are to apologize for not spending much time with you in the past few months," he said, apparently having forgotten they were surrounded by two dozen ladies who were soaking up every word so they could retell the story later in excruciating detail. "I've been working a lot. Overtime at the music store, then taking every weekend gig my band could book."

He shifted, apparently finding the hardwood floor uncomfortable against his denim-clad knee, and once again focused his gaze intently on Chelsea who seemed confused that his speech wasn't going where she had anticipated.

"I've been trying to put aside some money to provide for you and the baby. I can't afford the kind of things you're used to, and I'll probably never be on the cover of *Forbes* magazine," he said with a slight chuckle, "but I can promise that you and the baby will be rich in all the love I have to give you both."

His elderly aunt squelched her hearing aid and leaned closer to hear all that was transpiring between the two.

Mary, on the other hand, had tuned in to the memory of his surreptitious scribbling when she and Daisy had gone into the music store and she'd shown him her identification. Had he been writing down her information when she briefly turned her attention to Daisy? And was the credit card how he'd been attempting to provide for Chelsea and the baby?

The thought of such a possibility made her sick with anxiety. A mere ten minutes earlier, Chelsea had mentioned that Darius had brought the crib over and set it up for her. Could the crib have been in the large box the mystery person had picked up from her house? For that matter, she had been unsure whether the beat-up old SUV had been a charcoal or faded navy color, but it could as easily have been the dusty brown vehicle Darius had driven here today.

He cleared his throat to finish his speech. "Even though I can't promise you a lot of fancy stuff, I want to marry you and love you for the rest of my life. Chelsea"—he tugged earnestly at her hand—"will you marry me and make me the happiest man on earth?"

The room went quiet as all waited breathlessly for her answer. All Mary heard was the sound of her own heartbeat pounding in her ears.

"It's about time," said the outspoken aunt whose voice was stronger than her hearing. Then, in a slightly lower decibel, she added to the person next to her, "He got the sequence wrong. It's supposed to be marriage, then—"

Her companion shushed her so everyone could hear Chelsea's answer.

The cloud of sadness that had hung over the young mother-to-be when the father of her child had been noticeably absent earlier now dissipated, and a sunny smile brightened her features over the happy turn of events.

"Darius, I love you more than you will ever know. . . ."

Mary and the others held their breaths. Was there a "but" coming?

"And I would be thrilled to be your wife. Yes!"

Darius stood and swooped her up into his arms.

"Yes, yes, yes!" she cried, as if there were any lingering doubt as to her answer.

Like the ending of a cheesy movie, all the well-wishers in the room erupted into applause for the happy couple. Even Darius's aunt, who had disagreed with the timing of events, clapped enthusiastically for them, and Chelsea's ten-year-old cousin joined the excitement by hugging them around the waist.

Mary, standing quietly amid the fervor of family and friends, wrung her hands in silent concern. After a moment, she hesitantly joined in the applause.

SEVENTEEN

◆◆◆

Betty's car started easily, for which Mary was grateful. It was interesting how life's trials made a person more appreciative of simple blessings. At one point, she had wished for seat warmers in her next car. Now she just wished for a car that started on cue and took her where she wanted to go.

That simple wish awaited her at Honest Wayne's, where her Impala sat on the lot awaiting the final payment for the repairs that had been performed on it. She'd already made a couple of small payments, but a nice lump sum provided by the refinancing loan would be ideal if she wanted to take the car home before spring flowers started blooming.

During the time she'd been at the shower, a thin film of ice had formed on the surface of the water in the bottle she'd opened a couple of hours ago and left in the car. Mary leaned forward to adjust the heat, and the beginning of a tension headache grabbed her from the top of her head down to her knotted shoulders.

While the car finished warming up where it was parked in front of Chelsea's grandmother's house, Mary unearthed a bottle of aspirin from her purse and washed two of them down with what was left of the water in the bottle.

She put the cap back on the bottle, and stared at it, looking through it more than at it.

Ropinirole. Wayne had mentioned that the medication hadn't helped. Something nudged her to go to him and offer the suggestion that had just come to mind. It was something of a stretch, but it might be worth mentioning. Couldn't hurt. And it might even help.

The dealership was not on her way home, but she decided a quick visit to Honest Wayne's was in order anyway to discuss matters regarding the Impala.

When she arrived, the lot fairly teemed with people eager to spend their early-filed tax refunds on a new ride. After she parked Betty car's in a customer parking slip, she found Wayne hobbling on crutches at the far corner of the lot, opening the driver's-side door on a late-model blue car and pointing out the features to a young couple. When she caught his eye, he nodded and indicated he would be with her in just a moment.

As promised, a couple of minutes later, he left the couple to inspect the car further and discuss their decision privately.

"Ready to pick up your car?" he asked. His eyelid twitched as though it were dancing a rumba all by itself. Wayne motioned to the lot where she stood. "Or are you contemplating something a little newer?"

She dipped her head, hating to bring this up. She felt like a schoolgirl who had forgotten to turn in her homework and now needed to explain herself to the teacher.

"I just wanted to let you know I'm planning to pick up the car before too much longer. I'm just waiting on some paperwork to get straightened out so I can get the rest of the money to you."

It had been about two and a half weeks since the car had been towed in, and coordinating rides was getting old. If the refinancing was delayed much longer, she should probably consider renting a car and take some of the burden of her transportation off her friends and family. But the rental fee would provide even further challenges.

"No problem," he said. "Take as long as you need."

Another customer hovered nearby, and Wayne slanted his gaze at Mary as if to ask whether there was something else she needed from him.

"There is one other thing," she said. She pulled her coat tighter around her and tucked her chin against the stiff breeze that blew in off the bay.

Wayne leaned on his crutches and gave her his full attention.

"This may be none of my business, and if it isn't, please say so."

He lifted an eyebrow. Curiosity and a hint of concern flickered across his drawn face, but he merely waited for her to say what was on her mind.

"You had left a prescription in one of the books you traded at the bookshop."

"Oh, I thought I said you could throw it away."

"I did." She could tell he was starting to become impatient, so she would make it quick. "And then you said you broke your kneecap after falling out of bed."

Wayne nodded. He frowned a little, clearly trying to follow why she would bring this up now. "That's right. Worst case of jimmy legs ever."

The information sheet she'd picked up at the pharmacy had indicated the medicine's primary use was for Parkinson's disease, a degenerative condition known by its muscle tremors. But the medication was also commonly prescribed as an off-label solution for restless legs syndrome, hence Wayne's jimmy legs and resulting broken kneecap.

"I've suffered my share of charley horses," she confessed. "Taking magnesium or soaking in Epsom salts before bed always helps my muscles relax, and I thought it might help you too."

Wayne blinked, though she wasn't sure whether it was in response to her unsolicited suggestion or an attempt to still the weird twitch under his eye. "Thanks," he said. "I'll give it a try."

She wished it were as easy to take away the nervous tension that had disturbed her sleep since first learning an impostor had opened a credit account in her name. Unfortunately, the tension she now experienced went so deep that she doubted that any amount of Epsom salts would help.

No, she wouldn't sleep well until the Mary Fisher impersonator was exposed and paid for the crime.

———

At home that evening, Mary decided to change into her pajamas a little early. Most nights, when she shed her clothes and stepped into her warm flannels, it felt as if she were shedding the day's cares and concerns and stepping into a place of mellow relaxation. Exactly what she needed this evening. Tonight, she would spend some quality time with Betty, then turn in early. Although physically tired from the day's events, the emotional fatigue that accompanied the discoveries she'd made accounted for most of her desire to get to bed early.

Gus picked his way through her bedroom like a soldier treading around land mines—an insult, considering how clean and tidy the room was—and paused at the clothes she'd dropped on the floor. He sniffed the khaki slacks, then turned his furry face to Mary and squint-blinked several times to indicate his displeasure at the scent she had picked up while away for the afternoon.

"Oh, quit the theatrics," she said. "It was just a dog. And a cute one at that. But not as cute as you, of course."

He seemed unconvinced that her loyalty remained with him.

She picked up the clothes, removed the belt from the pants and emptied the pockets, then tossed the laundry in the hamper. As so often happened at the end of the day, she sorted through the loot that her clothes had offered up. Years ago, her son's pockets had yielded everything from rocks and string to bolts and batteries. Her daughter's pockets had contained game pieces, notes from friends, and lip balm. Every item told a story. There was no telling what the items in her own pockets told about her.

She moved to the wastebasket to drop in the scrap of paper she'd rescued from Pogo's jaws, then stopped herself. Frozen in midmotion, she stared at the paper in her hand.

Obviously intrigued, Gus stood on his hind legs and reached up to try to bat the paper out of her hand.

Her gaze still fixed on the remnant of mailing label, she sat down on the bed. Determined to win this game, Gus followed her up onto the coverlet and stretched out his nose. Mary, in turn, leaned away from the curious, whiskered face and rolled across the bed, laughing at his persistence.

Finally, in a reverse-psychology move, she crumpled the paper and tossed it to him. Gus levitated in place, sniffed the balled-up paper, and turned his back to her.

She could take the hint. He only wanted to play the game according to his rules. She grabbed the wadded paper and turned her focus back to what had caught her attention in the first place. Something on the address label.

Not much beyond the city and zip code remained. With only that information to go on, Mary picked up her laptop computer and turned it on.

Gus, thoroughly disinterested by now, jumped off the bed and stalked to the door to peer downstairs, presumably checking out the noises Betty was making as she puttered around downstairs.

Remembering the ZIP code map on the post office wall, she speculated the same information might be available online and entered ZIP plus four lookup in the search engine. From there, she clicked on the link and typed in her own address.

All nine digits matched.

Downstairs, a cabinet door opened, then banged shut. Lured by the prospect of a fishy treat, Gus flipped his bushy tail and went downstairs.

"Fickle," she called after him.

Next, she typed in Patsy Lambert's address. The first five zip code numbers were the same as her own, but the final four differed. A sickening feeling gripped the pit of her stomach at the confirmation that this package—whatever it had contained—had been addressed to Mary's neighborhood, not to Patsy's address. Nor had it been mailed to Darius, who lived on the same block as Chelsea's grandmother. The Mac computer in the baby's nursery, from the Apple store, perhaps? And then there was that Elsa Peretti silver spoon—most likely the Tiffany & Co. purchase credited to the account opened under her name.

Combined with the evidence, albeit weak, from the baby shower, this clinched her suspicion of Darius. Just before his proposal, he had mentioned being worried about keeping Chelsea in the manner to which she was accustomed. Had the pricey gifts been his way of trying to compete with her upper-crust upbringing?

Betty's voice drifted to her from downstairs. "Would you like a bowl of fresh fruit?"

Mary got up and paced the length of the room before answering. "In just a few minutes. I'm going to Skype Daisy first."

After going back to the computer, she opened it to the program that would allow her to talk to her granddaughter and see her face at the same time. She could sure use a pick-me-up right now.

She just hoped that she connected with Daisy at the other end, and not Aster.

The face on the screen smiled back at her. "Hi, Grandma!"

Daisy appeared happy, not desperate in the way she'd been during her two-week visit to Ivy Bay. And, unlike her time as the pretender who had called herself Aster, the tone of her conversation was relaxed and natural.

After the introductory chitchat was over, the girl leaned in and touched some computer keys. A second later, a cartoon rendition of a princess crown appeared over the image of her head on the screen. As she moved, the crown moved with her, always hovering above her head.

Mary leaned back and considered this latest development. She hoped this wasn't another manifestation of the Aster alter ego.

Daisy fidgeted with the keyboard again and laughed. More like a snort, actually. The princess crown disappeared as easily as it had appeared and, instead, a pair of pilot's goggles settled over her eyes. Then she performed a pantomime of a crazy head-banging rock performance, and once again, the cyber artwork followed her motions across the screen.

Mary laughed, and her sudden reaction surprised even herself. Just as she had hoped, her spontaneous granddaughter had lifted her spirits. "How did you do that?"

Daisy tilted her head and shrugged, and the goggles shifted to fall over her eyes at the proper angle. "It's just a fun little bonus on Skype."

Mary followed her instructions and played with the various drawings available to personalize one's features. The small inset of her own image on the laptop screen showed a gray-haired grandmother in a turban, followed by kitty ears and whiskers, and finally a medieval helmet with the face shield flipped up to show her eyes.

The novelty over, she turned her attention back to her granddaughter and the purpose of the call. "How's school going?"

"Let's just say I'm glad I put the time in on my term paper while I was at your house. Ever since we went back to school, all the teachers have loaded us up with homework as penance for taking those two weeks off."

Mary laughed again. She much preferred this kind of dramatic storytelling over the strange drama that had swirled around the persona that Daisy called Aster. "Before I forget, I found your iWatch at the bookshop."

Daisy twisted her mouth and gnawed the inside of her cheek. "Oh, that. There's really no such thing as an iWatch. It's just an old iPod Nano that I tried to turn into a status symbol."

This reiterated what Ashley had told her, and Mary appreciated Daisy's honesty. "I'll pop it in the mail to you," she said. The balloon-covered padded envelope at the post office would be put to use sooner than originally anticipated.

Daisy smiled back at her from the computer screen. "If you leave it at your house, that'll give me an excuse to come back and visit you sooner."

"It's a deal," Mary said, and they talked about the possibility of a long visit this summer. It made her feel good to know that her sweet granddaughter still wanted to spend time with her.

Daisy abruptly switched the subject in the way teenagers are known to do. "I met a cute boy at our church youth group," she said, bubbling over with enthusiasm. "He seems to like me."

Something in her tone made Mary take notice. "Why do you sound so surprised?"

"I looked all gross and ugly that evening. *Grugly*," she said, and giggled at the made-up word. "I was wearing plain jeans and one of my old tops, and my hair was pulled back in a half ponytail because I didn't have time to fix it up. You know what, Grandma? I was having a grunge day, but he didn't care. He thinks I'm cool."

In Mary's opinion, her granddaughter couldn't look grugly if she tried. "You *are* cool," she said. "Because that's the way God made you."

Daisy smiled in response to the compliment. "And you know what else? Since the fancy clothes and la-di-dah hairstyles didn't make a difference to him, I put those designer tops in the charity bag for women who need nice interview clothes." She snapped her fingers. "Next thing you know, Morganna and the other girls all of a sudden wanted me to do more stuff with them."

"That's great."

A sour expression crossed Daisy's pretty face. "It would be if I still wanted to be in their clique. But I'm more comfortable with my regular girlfriends. By the way, Grandma, you don't need to call me Aster anymore."

Not that she ever had, but she wasn't going to quibble over technicalities. "I'm glad to hear it. I'm getting older, so it was getting too hard to remember what to call you."

Daisy laughed at the joke, then turned serious. "I got to thinking what you said about copying Jesus, and it hit me! I'm already a designer-brand Daisy because I was designed by God. And if I try to be like anybody else, I'll just be a poor-quality knockoff."

That was what she'd been trying to tell the girl while she was here, but Daisy phrased it so much better than she ever could. "You're top quality in my eyes."

"Thanks, Grandma." Daisy looked over her shoulder and called to someone in another room, "Okay, I'll be there in a minute." Turning back to the computer, she said, "Mom needs me."

Mary started to say good-bye, then remembered what she wanted to ask her granddaughter. "Before you go, can you tell me if you found any mail on the back deck while you were here?"

"Yes. It was that day I was at the house by myself and that mean mailman came. I didn't answer the doorbell, so he left a package on the chair out back."

Mary frowned. "I don't recall seeing a package."

"Really? I brought it inside and put it in the kitchen pantry where you and Aunt Betty keep the mail."

Now she was really confused. "We don't keep mail in the—" She cut herself off. The kitchen pantry was where Mary had stashed the mail after finding Katina leafing through it. "Thank you, Daisy. I'll go check there now."

They said their good-byes and disconnected the session, and Mary took a moment to clean up the folders in her e-mail program. A peek into the spam folder unearthed the missing credit reports she had ordered almost three weeks ago.

She took a moment to peruse the documents—a task made easy by the very few entries recorded to her records over the past years. There was no information on the forms that she didn't already know. If not for the recent falsified account, she would have had a near-perfect rating.

Wanting to put that behind her for now, she closed the laptop and went downstairs to find Gus winding himself around Betty's legs in hopes of another treat. Dodging the persistent feline, her sister set two bowls of sliced bananas and berries on the table. A small dish of homemade granola had been set on the table as an optional topping for the berries.

"Thank you, Betty. That looks delicious. I hope the old wives' tale isn't true that bananas before bed make you have strange dreams."

"I don't see how they can get any stranger than some of the doozies you tell me about."

"Point taken." Mary walked over to the pantry and peered in.

"Looking for powdered sugar?"

"No." She checked the shelf where she had temporarily stored the mail basket. Nothing. "Daisy said she put a package in here."

"Why would she do that? We usually put the mail in that basket on the little table in the living room."

"She stuck it in here for safekeeping." Mary leaned in and poked around behind the stash of paper grocery bags. "Aha. Here it is. It must have fallen off the shelf."

She carried it to the table where Betty had already made herself comfortable. Her sister handed her the knife she'd used to cap the strawberries.

"Thanks." Mary cut the tape on the box and pulled out a Coach diaper bag.

"Oh my," said Betty. "It looks as though our mailman told you the truth."

Indeed he had. Now any remaining doubts she'd had about the irascible postal carrier had vanished.

After the berries were eaten and dishes put away, Betty moved to the living room where she opened a catalog and studied it intently. Sitting on the back of the couch, Gus licked a paw and washed his face.

Mary took a closer look at what her sister was reading. A seed catalog. Daisy had teased about such an activity being the epitome of a boring life, but Mary knew her sister enjoyed planning her garden each year.

Betty looked up and caught her smiling. From the knowing look she cast, it appeared she remembered Daisy's comment too. "Don't worry. I'll try to hold down the party noise over here."

With the laptop open on her knees and the Coach diaper bag beside her, Mary logged on to the Internet. All suspect arrows pointed to Darius in neon lights. The new guitar he had played at the Winter Carnival fund-raiser, and the shiny leather jacket he wore. Possibly a coincidence. But the large box—about the size of an unassembled crib—had been picked up by him or someone who drove an SUV just like his. And, of course, there were the items in the nursery and his insecurity about providing for Chelsea in the manner to which she was accustomed.

Determined to get this matter cleared up once and for all, she went to the bank's Web site to see what else she could find out about the account. Although a hold had been placed on it, the account had not been deleted since money was still owed. If possible, she'd like to take a peek and make sure no new charges had been added.

Reading from the statement she'd been given at the bank, she typed in the customer account number.

A box popped up, asking her to enter the password.

She sighed. Where to start?

A closer look revealed a clickable link in small print: Forgot Your Password? Not exactly, since she'd never supplied a password in the first place, but she clicked it anyway.

In response, the customer-generated security question asked, "What was the name of your first girlfriend?"

Mary leaned back against the sofa pillows and considered the implications behind that question. The credit account had been opened a little over a month ago, when Darius was less than two months away from becoming a father.

She shook her head. It was a bad sign that he was thinking of an old girlfriend while opening a credit card with stolen identity to provide for his pregnant fiancée. So many layers of negativity had been woven together in what was turning out to be a hangman's noose for the young man.

A memory tickled at the back of her mind. Could he have been so blatant as to name his band—Destiny's Pride— after a first love? On a hunch, she typed Destiny into the box displayed on the screen.

Fail. The computer instructed her to try again. Or, as an option, it offered to text the password to the cell phone number on file.

Regrettably, the texted option wouldn't do her any good. Worse, the text would only serve to warn the identity thief that someone was trying to access the account. And that might prompt him to change the password before she could figure it out.

So she typed in the next most logical word: his fiancée's name. Unfortunately, Chelsea as a password also failed. This was her second try, and a message warned that a third unsuccessful attempt would lock her out.

The next one had to work. With the pressure on, Mary laid her head back against the couch and closed her eyes. Images of the baby shower—when she had firmly connected the credit card to Darius—swirled through her mind.

Gifts. People. Varied conversations. She didn't bother to sort them; she just let them flow in random order, revealing everything and nothing.

And then something clicked.

Taking her third and final try, she entered a name. This time the account let her in.

With a catch in her breath, Mary stared at the screen, heartsick to discover her suspicion was correct.

EIGHTEEN

◆◆

There was a whole lot of praying going on at church the next morning, most of it coming from Mary. After silent prayer time, Betty had to nudge her to remind her to open her eyes and stand up while the congregation sang "Trust and Obey."

Reflecting on the song's lyrics, Mary knew that was exactly what she needed to do. Now that she had pieced together who the credit card culprit was, her beseeching prayers had been a request for God to convince her that if she followed through with bringing the criminal to justice that all would go well for everyone involved. But that information wasn't for her to know just yet. What she needed to do, as the song reminded her, was obey God in seeking out the truth and then trust Him to see it through to its best conclusion.

After the song, she sat down on the cushioned pew and stared straight ahead while Pastor Miles flipped pages in his Bible to find the right verse.

"You okay?" Betty whispered.

Mary shook her head. "Not really. It's hard to expose someone as a criminal and turn them over to the authorities.

That's why I was praying so hard. To make sure I'm doing the right thing. Not being hasty."

"It's the right thing, and I believe you're going about it the right way."

Her sister's vote of confidence helped quiet the nervous anxiety that made her want to just pretend she'd never discovered the information that had been revealed to her last night. Made her want to just let the investigators handle the matter so this person's arrest and subsequent criminal record would be on their hands and not hers.

Trust, she reminded herself, as Pastor Miles launched into the sermon. *And obey.* God is in control. All she had to do was give the information to Chief McArthur and let God and the law take care of the rest.

After the congregation was dismissed, Mary offered up one last request—that He comfort and guide the wrongdoer. Betty nudged her and pointed to the already-crowded aisle. "There's Chief McArthur. Better go catch him before he hightails it out of here."

Grateful for her sister's support, she gave Betty a spontaneous hug, then took off after the chief of police. Carefully sidestepping through the crowd so as not to crush any toes or knock an elderly parishioner off balance, she reached him before he exited the building. She touched his arm to gain his attention.

He turned, smiled, and said hello, then moved away as if to leave.

"May I speak with you for a minute?" The chief stopped to oblige, but she nodded toward the front door. "Privately?"

He dipped his head and sidled around the line that had formed to shake the pastor's hand. When Mary made her way outside, he was waiting for her near the parking lot.

To refresh his memory, she gave him a rundown of the credit card problem, then updated him on some of the newest developments. "I think I've pieced together who the culprit is."

She laid out the facts that had led to her conclusion and waited while he took it in.

"Nice work," he said, clearly impressed. "What's the name of that bank again? I'll get in touch with their fraud investigator before we decide on the next step."

Her hesitation must have shown, for he crossed his arms over his chest. "What now?"

"I was hoping to give the"—she looked around at the people who could accidentally overhear their conversation, not wanting to use the person's name and risking damage to their reputation on the slim chance that she might be wrong—"*suspect* a chance to do the right thing and own up to the crime. Maybe by doing so, this person could get a little leniency."

The last statement was her sincere request for the chief to consider the circumstances and perhaps go a little easy on the miscreant.

"Let me guess," he said. "You've got it all planned out."

She smiled for the first time that morning. "As a matter of fact, I do."

After she'd told him her plan, Mary watched the chief walk to his car. The comparison to *Gunsmoke*'s Matt Dillon hadn't been that far off the mark. His long, confident stride was eerily reminiscent of the fictional marshal's.

She considered starting the car to warm it up, but decided to wait by the sidewalk for Betty instead. A steady stream of people emerged from the church, but her sister wasn't among them. She must have gotten caught up talking to her sister-in-law Eleanor.

Henry strolled out of the church and peered into the sky as if trying to determine whether the distant clouds would become bothersome enough to keep him off his boat today. After he took his eyes off the clouds, he noticed her and crossed the yard to join her.

"Pretty day," he said. "Looks as if spring is trying to put in an appearance."

"By the calendar, it's almost another three weeks off. But speaking of spring, have you seen the flyers for the historic reenactments coming to Ivy Bay?"

"Ayuh. The events you're planning to stock the books for, eh?"

Mary pursed her lips and considered the possibility of that happening. "It depends on whether my credit situation gets resolved in time to place the orders."

The expression of remorse on his face couldn't have been more sincere if it had happened to him. "I was hoping the loan would have been approved by now."

The song they'd sung in church this morning echoed in her mind. Trust and obey. Well, she had obeyed by following through on her conversation with Chief McArthur. Now all that was left to do was trust that all would go according to God's plan. That knowledge perked her up more than any platitudes people might offer.

"Regardless of how the refinancing plays out," she said, "I'd still like to attend one or both of the reenactment events."

"That sounds like fun." He rubbed a hand across his jaw, and a scratching sound emanated from where his rough palm scraped across a spot he'd apparently missed while shaving this morning. "I love history. Watching the reenactments makes you feel as though you were right there, a hundred or more years ago."

Of course he loved history. It was one more of the many interests they shared. "Maybe we could go together," she said on an impulse.

He peered at her, his smiling eyes creating little "star rays," as Ashley called them. With a nod to indicate his pleasure at the prospect, he said, "It's a date!"

A date. After all the dread she'd experienced in facing her Cupid Couples date, followed by the sheer pleasure of spending time in this sweet man's company, his statement struck a silly chord in her, and a laugh popped out before she could stop it.

Apparently realizing what he had just said, Henry joined in the laughter and added, "on my calendar."

———

Monday's book club meeting turned out to be a bittersweet one. Sadness permeated the group as they realized that, with two members close to delivering and another moving away from Ivy Bay at the end of the school year, the young mothers would no longer have the time or opportunity to continue their book discussions.

On the other hand, so many blessings had come out of their gathering to share ideas, voice opinions, learn, and grow. The primary blessing had been the formation of some solid friendships. Mary liked to think that whatever advice or timeless sayings she'd managed to convey to these lovely ladies would eventually be passed on to their children. And their children's children. When she thought about it, it was really rather impressive to consider how far the ripples could flow from even one kind word or offer of a helping hand.

After the closing prayer—the group's final good-bye—Tamera motioned for Mary to put aside gathering up her belongings and remain seated. "We have something for you."

Mary took the card and gift the young woman handed her and let her gaze sweep over the cluster of new friends that she wanted to keep forever.

"What's this about? You didn't need to give me anything." Didn't need to, but they obviously had wanted to. Anticipatory smiles let Mary know they had treasured their time together as much as she had.

"Open it," said Kaitlyn. Her eagerness ran as high as if the gift were intended for her.

While the four of them looked on, Mary lifted the attractive homemade card out of its envelope. On the front, six words had been written in an elegant calligraphy script: *Mary's Top Ten Words of Wisdom*. And inside, artfully cut scraps of colorful paper served as backdrops for short blurbs and their correlating verses from the book of Matthew, chapters six and seven:

1. *Do the right things for the right reasons.*
2. *Pray God's agenda, not yours.*
3. *Forgive others.*
4. *Prioritize eternal things, not temporary ones.*
5. *Don't worry.*
6. *Seek the Kingdom first.*
7. *Don't judge others.*
8. *Ask, and it will be given.*
9. *Stay true to your convictions.*
10. *Obey God.*

"Oh my. I don't know what to say." To think that they had distilled these bits of understanding from their many conversations was enough to make her weep with joy.

She reached into her sweater pocket, but Kaitlyn beat her to the punch and handed her the box of tissues that had sat at the ready for every book club discussion. The once-full box was now half empty. Mary took two and dabbed at the moisture that had collected in the corners of her eyes.

"Thank you so much," she said. "This is so very touching."

Tamera pointed to the unopened gift. "Full disclosure time. This is from all of us, but Brianna did most of the work on it. Mainly because she's better at it than we are. But we all pitched in on the materials."

Mary appreciated the girl's complete honesty and worked hard to suppress a grin of amusement.

Brianna, on the other hand, reacted in her usual shy manner to being thrust in the spotlight. "Everybody had an equal part," she said softly and lifted a hand to her collar.

"I certainly appreciate the thought." Mary removed the paper and pulled out a knitted item made of variegated shades of bold pink and navy blue yarn. Unable to discern what the lovely handcrafted item might be, she was tempted to ask, but stopped herself. The soft crescent-shaped piece sported a pretty button on one end and a loop on the other. Whatever it happened to be, the colors were lovely and, unlike her own fumbling lack of knitting skills, the needlework displayed in it was excellent.

"It's a neck warmer," Chelsea offered. "For those times when it's a little chilly inside, but not enough to put on an extra sweater." She grinned. "And it'll keep your voice warmed up for those times when you have more words of wisdom to share."

The waterworks started anew at the thought and effort they had put into this gift. Unable to stay seated, Mary rose to her feet and thanked them profusely for the gift, and most of all for the gift of their friendship. Hugs were dispensed with abandon.

"Please stop by the bookshop whenever you can," she urged. "You don't need to buy anything. Just pop in to say hello and let me know how you're doing."

After promising to visit, the girls picked up their belongings to leave, and Mary began stuffing the books and reference materials she'd brought into her tote bag.

The door swung open, and Chief McArthur strode in, his chest thrust forward and his hands near his belt like an old western lawman about to reach for his six-shooter. A serious expression clouded his otherwise attractive features.

"Mrs. Mary Nelson Fisher?" he asked in a somber tone and stared directly at her.

"Of course I'm Mary Fisher." She laughed nervously under his unblinking gaze. "Why are you asking me that? You know who I am."

"Turn around and place your hands on top of your head," he ordered.

NINETEEN

＊

W-what?" Mary sputtered. "I—"

The girls all froze like rock statues in shocked reaction to the drama unfolding before them.

"Just do as I said, ma'am," Chief McArthur insisted and withdrew a pair of handcuffs from his back pocket. "You're under arrest for credit card fraud and felony theft. You have the right to remain silent. Anything you say can and will be used against you in a court of law—"

Cold metal clamped around Mary's right wrist, and he pulled both hands down to secure them behind her back.

"Please let me go," she pleaded. "This must be a mistake! I didn't have anything to do with credit card fraud."

Tamera, the oldest, was the first to speak up. "You must have the wrong Mary Fisher," she insisted. "Our mentor would never break any laws."

"Step back, please," Chief McArthur instructed.

The girl wisely did as she was told, but Mary was a little less reticent about standing her ground, even though her hands were bound behind her back. "But I didn't do anything. Tell me what this is all about."

"You should have done better research when you planned your scheme," he said with a slight sneer. "Anyone with any street savvy at all knows that when someone with a new credit card bill and a high balance claims to have had their identity stolen, the first place investigators look is to the owner of the credit card. You, Mrs. Fisher," he said, clamping on the left wrist cuff and turning her to face him, "will not get away with the spending spree you've perpetrated over the past six weeks."

He let his gaze roam around the room as if daring anyone to challenge him, then turned his focus back to Mary.

"I suggest you let your family know you won't be coming home for dinner tonight. And many more nights after that."

Mary tested the strength of the cuffs, but the hard, cold metal wouldn't budge. One of the quotes from the card burned in her brain: *Pray God's agenda, not yours.* Her heart pounded, unsure what would happen next and praying that God would take the situation under His control.

Until today—until this very moment—Chelsea had remained poised and smoothly confident in the book club and in all her dealings with others. But now, for the first time since Mary had known her, the young woman's composure crumbled.

Chelsea lunged forward and tried to pull Chief McArthur's guiding hand away from Mary's elbow. "Don't arrest her!" she insisted. "Let her go."

Chief McArthur, however, had been trained for times such as this, and he quickly blocked the move. "Ma'am, don't make me restrain you," he said, the warning in his voice chilling.

At that, Chelsea broke into tears. Not just a dainty little trickle, but a gully washer of water flowed down her pretty face. She lifted her wrists to the officer. "Then do it. Arrest me."

"What's going on in here?" Katina Stanley marched into the room like a dictator demanding answers from the commoners. She sized Chief McArthur up and down, then held out her hand, palm up. "Search warrant, please."

If Mary weren't already at the chief's mercy, she might have been intimidated by the commanding note in Katina's voice.

He scowled at the human dynamo. "I don't need a search warrant," he explained slowly and carefully, as if talking to a small child. "I've got an arrest warrant."

He waved a piece of paper, then shoved it back in his pocket before returning his attention to Mary. He gave her a firm nudge in the direction of the door.

Not about to give him reason to slap on more charges, Mary quietly obliged. Apparently unwilling to risk making things worse, the other girls had given wide berth to the dramatic action unfolding before them.

Katina, on the other hand, had other ideas. "I will not have you coming in here and—"

"I said, just do it," Chelsea insisted and again pushed her slim wrists toward him. By now, she had regained some of her composure, despite the continuing flow of tears. "Arrest me. Mary didn't do anything. She doesn't know anything about the credit card."

All heads turned to Chelsea.

"What are you saying?" Katina demanded.

"I'm saying Mary didn't open that credit card, and she didn't order any merchandise." The girl looked beseechingly at Mary, asking without words for undeserved forgiveness. "I did it. I opened the card, and I ordered all that stuff."

"You?" Brianna said. Pain filled her eyes, and when she self-consciously reached for her collar, the heart necklace bobbed under the movement.

"I'm so sorry," Chelsea said, her head bowed in submission before Mary. "I didn't know you when I used your information to open the credit card. Your name and data were just words on an application that I saw on the secretary's desk out front."

"You went through my papers?" Now that the shoe had been jammed on the other foot, Katina finally understood how offensive it was when others violated certain boundaries.

And then the real truth came out.

"After I got to know you, I didn't tell you because I just assumed that you wouldn't be affected by it. I was hoping that once you found out about it, you'd tell the credit card company you didn't make those charges. Which is what you did."

Stunned by the audacity of it all, Mary could barely speak. By now, she barely noticed the handcuffs digging into her wrists. "What did you think they would do with all those charges, Chelsea? Someone had to pay for all that stuff."

Chelsea shrugged and sniffed. "I thought the credit card company would merely close the account and absorb the loss as a business write-off. I had no idea you'd be arrested!"

The tears started anew, and Chief McArthur unlocked the cuffs to release Mary from the unwelcome restraint. She rubbed where the hard metal had pinched the skin.

"Now that I know you'll be stuck having to pay for all that stuff and serve time for fraud, I feel just terrible for putting you—my *friend*—in this terrible spot." She reached out to Mary. "Please forgive me. I never meant to hurt you."

Apparently forgetting the *don't judge others* bit of wisdom they'd been taught, Kaitlyn said, "Why would you even need to steal? Your parents are filthy rich."

Chelsea pulled a tissue from the box and wiped away the mascara streaks that marred her face. She simply shook her head. "You wouldn't understand."

A surge of compassion flooded through Mary, and she opened her arms to the young woman who was clearly remorse-stricken. Like a mother correcting her own child, Mary kept her voice firm but kind, and her embrace forgiving.

"This is what we meant about prioritizing eternal things," she said. "People before things, and God highest of all."

"I know that now," Chelsea said, her voice muffled against Mary's shoulder. "But at the time, it seemed so important that I have that stuff. For the baby, you know? And for Darius."

Chief McArthur moved in to break up the moment of reckoning. "Get your things," he instructed. "You need to come with me."

Chelsea turned her face to Mary, questioning what she should do now.

"Go with the chief," she said, "and I'll call your grandmother."

"Please break it to her gently. She's been so good to me. I feel bad for causing her more trouble. And you."

"You just focus on making things right, and we'll be here to support you."

The girls all murmured their agreement.

Mary made it clear she held no grudge against Chelsea and added, "We'll work this out."

"Why would you want to?"

She took Chelsea's hand and patted it to convey the sincerity she found hard to express in words. "Because you're worth it."

Katina, who'd been taking it all in, now spoke up and addressed Chief McArthur, who stood at the ready to escort Chelsea out to his police car. "You're not thinking of walking an eight-and-a-half-months pregnant woman through my lobby in those handcuffs, are you? I won't have it."

"I don't think I have to worry about her running away." With a pointed stare at his charge, he asked, "Do I, Chelsea?"

The girl looked down at her cumbersome belly and sadly shook her head.

Although the situation was a sad one, Mary was glad it had worked out the way she'd hoped. When she had unfolded her plan to Chief McArthur yesterday, she had elicited a promise that he'd go easy on the girl if she confessed. Which, thank goodness, she had. Even so, Mary's heart felt heavy with the burden that this sweet girl had succumbed to temptation and gone so far astray. She would keep Chelsea in her prayers and ask God to help the young woman get her priorities—eternal priorities—straightened out in time to teach them to her child.

The police chief closed his hand around Chelsea's upper arm and steered her toward the door. As he was about to exit, he turned back to Mary and tipped his hat. "Nice job," he mouthed.

Katina followed the pair out of the room, presumably to supervise the escort from the premises, but Mary supposed the nurse-practitioner was more intent on diverting waiting patients' attention away from the drama taking place in her clinic.

Tamera, Kaitlyn, and Brianna milled around the room, apparently at odds as to what they should do now. What they should say.

Mary filled the stunned silence. "People make mistakes. We learn from them and move on. Our job right now is to forgive the offense and love the offender."

Kaitlyn flipped a tendril of hair over her shoulder. "You're nicer than I would be if she did that to me."

She and Tamera grabbed their things and said their good-byes, leaving Brianna lingering behind with Mary. The young woman's hand once again went to her collar, but this time, she reached behind her neck and removed the necklace.

She held it out to Mary.

"What's this for?"

Brianna looked down at the floor. "It was a friendship gift from Chelsea. Now that I know how she bought it, I can't keep it." She placed the necklace in Mary's hand.

It was the same Elsa Peretti open heart design she'd seen that day in Tiffany & Co. and again on the silver spoon the day of Chelsea's baby shower.

"You might want to see if you can return it for credit," Brianna suggested.

Mary's heart surged with affection for this precious young woman. Although her family situation was unfortunate, with her parents turning their backs on her for having gotten pregnant outside of marriage, Brianna seemed to have her head screwed on straight. Once she made a new start as a nanny for the family that had decided to hire her, Mary felt certain her baby would have the stability and acceptance that Brianna herself had not.

"Thank you," Mary said. She gave her young friend another hug and wished her well. "I meant what I said about staying in touch."

TWENTY

———◆◆◆———

Two days later, history seemed to be repeating itself as Henry bowed and motioned Mary into his car. "My chariot awaits you."

On the road to Honest Wayne's Auto Sales and Repair, he expressed his sympathy for her having gone so long without wheels. "It must have been hard having to depend on others to take you where you wanted to go."

"It was humbling," she admitted. "Not a bad thing, though. It reminded me what a blessing it is to have the freedom to get up and go wherever I please, whenever I please. I'll appreciate that blessing even more whenever I start up my Impala and the engine runs smoothly."

"Now that your car is fixed and ready to be picked up, I take it you finally got your loan approved?"

She put on her sad face. "The bad news is that so much time passed between the application and approval that the interest rate changed."

He threw her a look of empathy. "That's a shame. I know you were looking forward to saving money by locking in on a lower refinance rate."

Now she grinned to let him know she'd been pulling his leg. "I wouldn't call it a shame, especially since the rate *dropped*, which means my payments will be lower than anticipated and I'll save even more money in the long run." She clapped her hands with excitement.

Henry lifted a thumb in salute to her good fortune. "Nice going. You're like that guy in the parable who invested his ten talents and was blessed for being a good steward of his master's money." After a moment, he turned serious. "Have you heard anything from Chelsea?"

The remainder of his question hung unspoken between them: *since her arrest.*

"She was released. The last I heard, her parents have arranged to pay the bill for her."

Henry looked at her in a way that let her know he was wondering the same thing. By bailing Chelsea out of trouble, were the parents enabling her to continue making similar choices in the future? Were they teaching her that her bad decisions could be wiped away with their signature on a check?

Mary had only told him about the arrest but hadn't had a chance to fill him in on how she had come to suspect Chelsea. He already knew about the stakeout, but now she revealed it had been Darius who had come to her home to pick up the large box—a baby crib—at Chelsea's request.

"I found out after the fact that Darius had been unaware of Chelsea's illegal spending spree. Apparently, she told him the crib had been dropped off at my house by mistake, and he didn't question it." She considered Darius's natural assumption that his girlfriend had made a legitimate request, and his quick willingness to help. "He seems like a good guy. I hope this doesn't end their relationship."

She filled Henry in on her discovery of the items at Chelsea's grandmother's house that matched the purchases on the credit card.

"And then there was the new jacket that Darius wore the day of his performance at the Winter Carnival. And the brand-new guitar that was so shiny it looked like it had never been used before that day."

"Those could have been a coincidence," Henry said, pointing out the obvious.

"Exactly. That's what I thought at the time. But it turned out Chelsea had given them to him in an attempt to hold his interest. You see, he had been working overtime to try to put aside some money to provide for her and the baby. But when he received those expensive gifts from Chelsea, he thought he had to raise his game to be able to match her generosity. Which led him to work even harder and spend even less time with her."

"*Hmm*, not good. Sort of a warped version of 'The Gift of the Magi,'" Henry said, referring to the classic short story that captured the essence of irony.

"Of course, I couldn't be certain that the baby gifts she showed us in the nursery were the same ones that had been charged to the credit card, but the coincidences were very compelling."

"And you couldn't let it go until you knew for sure," he said.

"Absolutely." What was the use in denying it? He knew that she could be like a hungry dog with a juicy bone at times. "But the final clue—the one that redirected me from suspecting Darius to assuming Chelsea might be the culprit— was the security question on the bank's Web site."

Henry slowed for a young boy who chased a ball toward the road. The red rubber ball rolled to a stop in the ditch in front of the house and the child safely retrieved it, so Henry continued carefully on his way.

"Leave it to you to find a clue in a security question. After seeing a man retrieve the box from your house, what was it that led you to think a female—much less Chelsea—was the guilty party?"

She hadn't noticed it at first, but a tiny clue had given it away. "The space between 'girl' and 'friend.'"

Her friend rolled his eyes heavenward and laughed. "Of course! Now, why didn't I think of that?"

"As one word, it indicates a romantic relationship. But as two words, it refers to a friend who happens to be a girl. Since Amity, the girl who threw the baby shower for Chelsea, was her"—she used finger quotes as she'd seen Nathan Bayard do, but her version lacked his snarly attitude—"*best girl friend since kindergarten*, Amity was the password I entered, and it worked."

"That's pretty incredible. Way to go." He glanced over at her. "I have some good news for you."

"Great. I could use some good news." After trying to find out who had stolen her identity, followed by this week's disturbing turn of events that revealed her sweet young friend as the culprit, almost any news would sound good to her ears.

"The buzz at the post office is that the mail carrier you and Betty find so annoying is no longer temping for the postal service. Instead, he's moving to Boston to join an advertising firm there."

Mary hated to admit it, even to herself, but she did find a certain pleasure in knowing she and her sister wouldn't have to face that surly man again.

"Better than that, the routes will be adjusted so Bob Hiller will carry to your residential neighborhood until Rosalba returns from maternity leave."

Okay, her first reaction was a slightly selfish one, but she was glad she and Betty would experience Bob's sunny personality as he performed his job. But, truthfully, she was also glad for Nathan's return to the career he enjoyed. He clearly hadn't been happy delivering mail, so it was better that he returned to the profession that allowed him to create that mail.

"I hear your nurse friend raised a lot of money for the clinic," Henry said. He shot a playful wink at her. "I'm glad we were able to contribute our Cupid Couples registration fees to a good cause."

"Me too." Although Katina still disrespected the boundaries of others, she had a good heart and was fiercely protective of the patients in her care.

Henry slowed to turn into Honest Wayne's car lot, and Mary's thoughts naturally drifted to the salesman who, it turned out, did not have a gambling problem after all. In fact, his honesty may have been what had gotten him in trouble with that thug in Boston. Stranger still, she had reason to believe he'd been telling the truth about how he'd broken his kneecap.

Her chauffeur pulled up near the service entrance. Grateful for Henry's eagerness to help, and unwilling to inconvenience him any further, she thanked him for the ride and reached for the door handle before he could get out of the car and open it for her.

"Oh, Mary?" he said, stopping her hasty exit.

"Yes?"

He smiled, and his sea-green eyes shimmered with amusement. "I'm glad you're my girl-space-friend."

She returned his smile with one of her own and touched his hand where it rested on the gear shift. "Me too," she said. "Me too."

After waving good-bye to Henry, she glanced over at her car, which had been parked on the lot since the work on the transmission had been completed. It surprised her how happy she was to see the familiar car once again in good working order.

Inside, Wayne met her in the reception area and greeted her warmly. He was down to one crutch now and the black brace over his pant leg.

"Welcome!" he said. "We have just the car for you. A smooth-riding vehicle, well taken care of, and with reasonable mileage. You take this car home, and it'll serve you well for a nice long time."

He smiled so wide, he almost exposed his wisdom teeth. But despite his high-energy approach, he looked more rested than he had the last time she'd seen him. Not twitchy. And even though he had shifted into sales mode when she walked into the building, he didn't seem quite so high pressured and frantic as before.

Assuming the salesman must have forgotten why she had come today, she gently reminded him, "I'm here to pick up my Impala. Your service team replaced the transmission."

"Yes!" he agreed. "That's the new car I was telling you about. It drives like a dream. You'd never know that it's been around the block"—he shrugged—"eh, around Massachusetts a few times. You'll get quite a few more years out of it, if that's what you want. And if it's not, you know where to trade it in. Just come back here and talk to me. I'll find the exact car you want."

"Thank you so much. I'll be sure to do that when the time comes. Meanwhile, I appreciate your fast turnaround on the repairs."

Wayne dropped the salesman shtick, and a more serious demeanor took its place. "I should thank you," he said ever so sincerely.

"Me?" For bringing the car in? The reception room looked rather full, so he didn't seem desperate for business.

"Yes. For suggesting I ask my doctor about taking magnesium for my RLS. Because of you, my eye twitches are gone, my legs aren't running all night, and I'm sleeping much better. Even my doctor is impressed with the improvement."

In the past, Mary had taken magnesium after a day of rigorous physical activity that caused her calf muscles to cramp up. It pleased her to learn that her simple home remedy had given him relief.

"I'm glad it helped," she said.

"Well, why are we waiting around here? You have a car you want to pick up. Let's go get your paperwork."

He led her to his office and rummaged through the papers on his desk until he found hers, then motioned for her to take a seat.

"I also want to thank you for telling Chief McArthur about my, *um*, altercation in Boston a couple of weeks ago." He eased into the rolling chair, taking care not to bump his leg, and propped the crutch against the filing cabinet behind him.

Most men wouldn't appreciate her telling someone he'd almost gotten beat up. His comment surprised her, especially since she had feared he might have been involved in something either unethical or illegal.

"You see, I had arranged to buy some used cars from a dealer."

The car dealer Chief McArthur had cautioned her to avoid.

"Well, I was about to take delivery of them when I discovered they were illegally selling cars that had been flooded in Hurricane Sandy."

Mary nodded. "I saw a television exposé about disreputable car dealers selling vehicles that had been totaled because of water damage. The dealers paid junk prices for them, cleaned them up, and were passing them off to unsuspecting buyers as quality used cars." She thought about some of the victims of that crime who could barely afford the cars and certainly couldn't afford to replace them after the engines failed and the interiors molded. "The unknowing buyers got stuck with severely damaged cars."

"Yeah, that's what I'm talking about. Not the same guys, but the same scam." He pointed his finger at Mary. "And one of those cars was a newer-model Impala that I had planned to bring back for you to test-drive. When I realized what was going on and tried to back out of the deal, one of the sellers was, *ahem*, adamant that I fork over the money for those dud cars."

She leaned forward in her chair. "I was so worried he would hurt you if he caught you. That guy was *huge!*"

"No need for worry." He grinned, and the expression was much more attractive than his have-I-got-a-car-for-you face. "Skinny guys can run faster than beefcakes. It's pure physics." He laughed at his own humor. "But it helped that your shout distracted him and gave me a head start."

"I'm just relieved that we can laugh about it now."

"Anyway, I was debating what to do about those guys—they're bad news—when who should appear in my doorway but Ivy Bay's own chief of police."

If he hadn't already thanked her for mentioning the situation to Chief McArthur, she might have assumed his words were laced with sarcasm. As it was, he seemed genuinely happy that she had intervened on both counts—first, when she had shouted to him from across the street, and later, after she'd mentioned the incident to the police.

"That guy's a smart one," he said, referring to Chief McArthur. "He already knew about that shady business. I can't go into all the details, but he coordinated efforts with me and the Boston police to shut those guys down."

"That's wonderful. I hope they're permanently out of the used-car business." Meaning, she hoped they wouldn't be in a position to retaliate against Wayne for cooperating with police.

"That guy could have killed me if he'd caught me. I was lucky," he told her, "or maybe God was watching over me. But the good guys won, and I'm not hurt, other than my own clumsiness." He pointed down at his braced leg, as if she might not have figured out what he was talking about. "And the bad guys were put out of business. It's all good."

Indeed, it was. They both had a lot to be thankful for. He, for his improved health and new status as a hero for helping flush out some criminals who gave his business a bad name. And she, for her newly repaired car so she no longer needed to bum rides or borrow Betty's car.

She rose from the chair to shake Wayne's hand and once again noticed the small sterling-silver compass on a chain around his neck. She pointed to the piece. "With so many people using GPS devices in their cars these days, it won't be long before folks won't even remember what a compass is."

He came around his desk, propped himself against the crutch, and lifted the compass for her to take a closer look.

"I liked it because it reminded me of those older cars that had compasses built into the dash."

"It's quite unusual," she agreed.

Wayne nodded. "I bought it in Boston, at that fancy-dancy jewelry store that serves breakfast," he said, confirming her earlier discovery of the pendant during her visit to Boston with her family. "The one with the movie named after it."

Mary suppressed a grin after she realized he was talking about *Breakfast at Tiffany's*. "You mean Tiffany's?"

"Yes, that's the one. After Chief McArthur and I had corralled those criminals, I realized it has a deeper meaning." He breathed on the glass that protected the delicately balanced needle and buffed it against his shirt. "From now on, this compass will serve as a constant reminder to always choose 'true north' and continue building my good reputation in the community as an honest businessman."

Almost mindlessly, he rubbed a finger over the silver piece. His focus seemed to go back over the many customer interactions he'd had over the years.

"I want people to know me by my *sterling* reputation."

"That's a noble aspiration," she said. And she sincerely wished him well in his quest to live the life of an honorable man.

As for her, she had her own compass that pointed to true north: a black book called the Holy Bible.

TWENTY-ONE

◆◆◆

Patsy Lambert's church had been beautifully decorated with candles, flowers, floor runners, and ribbons on the pews. With all the attention to detail, the casual observer wouldn't know how hastily the celebration had been put together. Darius had insisted the wedding—now a mere week after his proposal—take place before the baby's birth. After Chelsea's confession, Mary's heart had been lifted that he was willing to give his fiancée another chance despite learning she'd bought all that merchandise with a fraudulent credit card, and not with her parents' money as he and others had assumed.

At the front of the church, the groom looked resplendent in his suit, and the bride absolutely glowed in the long flowing dress she'd borrowed from her grandmother.

Instead of launching into the presentation of rings, as was common at this point in the ceremony, Darius turned away from Chelsea and picked up a guitar that had been propped near the altar. The antiquated instrument's finish had been worn dull in spots, and various nicks and scratches marred the surface.

"I wrote this song for you," he said, gazing at his bride. "You were always in my thoughts, so whenever something came to me, I just stopped what I was doing and wrote down the lyrics." He chuckled. "My boss wasn't thrilled with me writing songs when there were customers in the store, but I couldn't stop myself."

So that was what Darius had been writing the day she and Daisy had gone to the music store where he worked. He hadn't been copying down her address and Social Security number, but jotting song lyrics for the woman he loved. Nudged by guilt for assuming the worst about the nice young man, Mary fidgeted on the pew next to Henry, who, lured by the promise of wedding cake and punch, had kindly agreed to accompany her as her "date."

Darius strummed the guitar, and it sounded amazingly good despite its scruffy appearance. "Nothing I write could ever be as pretty and special as you are."

A collective "aw" reverberated through the church. The groom sang straight from his heart, the words of the song expressing his undying love for both Chelsea and their as-yet-unborn baby. It was a sweet song and a sweet moment, one that seemed so very private despite the public setting.

The couple had written their own vows, which followed the heart-touching serenade. They weren't Shakespeare, but the messages were personal to them, and no one could deny their sincerity.

After the ceremony was over, she and Henry stayed for the reception, which included wedding cake from Sweet Susan's Bakery and photos of the happy couple.

Darius and Chelsea cut the cake, and Henry held Mary's purse while she angled the camera for a good shot. The couple offered cake to each other and giggled through bites of the tasty confection.

After serving began, Henry handed the purse back to her and nabbed two plates of the spice cake covered in cream frosting. "I'm glad they didn't smear cake all over each other like some couples do," he said, and passed her a plate. "Frosting in the face spoils the romance of the ceremony."

"You softy," she said, giving him a playful poke with her elbow. "Keep talking like that and I'll have to tell everyone that big, tough Henry gets mushy at weddings."

When he didn't respond to her gentle teasing, she turned and followed his gaze to the new husband and wife.

"I don't think she likes the cake," he said.

That might be an understatement. Chelsea's legs wobbled, and she wore an expression of embarrassment and physical discomfort.

"I think she's going to hurl." Henry put his plate down and scanned the reception hall. "Do you see a trash can anywhere?"

"No," she said in answer to his first statement. "She looks like she's in labor."

Mary moved through the crowd like a penny-pincher at a clearance sale. One minute she'd been happily gabbing with her friend, and the next, she stood over Chelsea who clutched the cake table for balance.

"Mary, it's so good to see you," the bride said, smiling through the pain. "Thank you for coming. And for not, you know."

Judging. "I wouldn't have missed your wedding for anything. How long have you been in labor?"

"A couple of hours. Maybe more. I read that your first baby can take a long time. So I kept it a secret from Darius because I didn't want him to worry."

Darius, who had until now turned away to speak to a wedding guest, apparently heard his name and looked over his shoulder at his wife. "What's going on?"

"Cramps."

At the same time, Mary said, "Labor."

His conversation with the guest forgotten, he grabbed Chelsea's arm as if he expected her to suddenly fall to the floor. "What do we do?"

Answering his own question, he retrieved a chair from the row by the wall and tried to get her to sit down.

"Do you need to lie down?" he asked. Panic filled his voice, and he turned one way, then the other, before looking to Mary for guidance.

"She needs to go to the hospital," she said, keeping her tone level and calm.

"You're joking, right? Chelsea hasn't thrown the bouquet yet." The young father clearly didn't understand that when it comes to childbirth, the baby is the one that sets the schedule.

Chelsea peeled his fingers off her arm, and the pink fingerprints that remained gave evidence of how nervous Darius was. "No, this is for real, honey. Maybe you should call someone."

He dug into his pocket, withdrew a cell phone, and punched in three numbers. "My wife is having a baby!" he yelled into the phone. "You've gotta come *now*."

Heads turned, and the crowd around the cake table quickly swelled.

The bride waited for Darius to give their address to the dispatcher, then said quietly, "I meant you should call our parents over here to let them know what's going on."

He looked frantically around the room, pulled at his hair, and finally retrieved his phone again. "I'll call them back and tell them not to send an ambulance."

Now Henry, who had been watching safely from the sidelines, spoke up. "No, let the professionals take care of her," he said, laying a hand on the younger man's shoulder. "Trust me."

"How appropriate," Rebecca said, and took the book order list from Mary. "Here it is, the first day of spring and we're finally ready to order new stock for the spring sidewalk sale." She looked down at the lengthy list. "That's a lot of books."

"Most of it is to replenish our regular inventory. The rest are split between books about the historical period of the reenactments and history mysteries."

The bell over the door interrupted their task, and four people entered. Five, if she counted the pink bundle in Chelsea's arms. Chelsea, Darius, and Chelsea's parents stepped into the shop. All glowed with happiness, but the parents appeared somewhat hesitant.

"Oh, what a cutie!" Mary said. For courtesy's sake, she waited through the introductions before cooing over the new arrival.

Rebecca came from behind the checkout counter. "Ooh, let me see the little munchkin!" With Chelsea's permission, she pulled back the blanket to examine the baby and made nonsense noises at her.

Mary shot her assistant a teasing grin. "Sounds like you're ready for a sibling for Ashley."

Rebecca waved her hand at Mary as if to dismiss the notion. "Why don't you take your friends to the back where you can sit and have a nice chat?"

"That's a lovely idea." To the two couples, she said, "Would you like some tea? We also have biscotti."

Her guests took off their coats and made themselves comfortable, the visiting ladies on the overstuffed chairs and Mary and the gentlemen on folding chairs that she had retrieved from the storage room.

"I could use a shot of caffeine to keep me awake," Chelsea said in answer to Mary's offer. "The baby doesn't understand our concept of days and nights yet."

"You have my sympathies. It's hard waking up several times a night and then trying to stay awake during the day to care for a little one."

After tea was served, Mrs. Lambert dabbed her lips and set down her cup on the small coffee table. "Mary, this isn't just a social visit. We stopped by today because we want to thank you for being so gracious about the, *er*, problem you were presented."

She seemed reluctant to even mention the crime. Mary didn't blame her. It must have been hard for the family to receive the news of what Chelsea had done.

Chelsea bounced the baby, who had begun to wriggle in her arms. "If it weren't for you asking for leniency for me, I most certainly would be separated from my husband and daughter while serving time for my bad decisions. But Chief McArthur seems to think the judge will give me a break if I can prove I'm trying to make things right."

At the words "serving time," Mrs. Lambert cringed involuntarily.

Whereas her mother had cringed at the words, Mary found Chelsea's directness encouraging. It sounded as though she wasn't trying to sweep her transgressions under a rug and pretend they had never happened. She seemed to fully understand just how far justice could be taken.

"It was your first offense," Mary said, "so I'm sure the judge will take that into consideration."

Chelsea nodded in affirmation, her dark hair brushing her daughter's head. "It was my first *and last* offense. I'll never do anything that stupid again."

Darius, clad in a faded jean jacket, leaned in and kissed his wife on the temple.

The young woman smiled at his attention. "My hearing will be coming up soon. To make sure the judge understands how serious I am about making things right, I've decided to start doing some community-service work. Katina said she'd be glad for some help at the clinic and would put in a good word for me, so I'll be putting in some hours over there."

Mrs. Lambert crossed her hands over her knees in a gesture that seemed more self-conscious than prissy. "I have to admit that we"—she nodded to her husband—"Chelsea's father and I, are partly to blame for what transpired."

A frown pulled at Mary's lips in response to the woman's statement. Chelsea had been owning her role in the identity theft and attempting to make some sort of restitution. She hoped the parents' indulgent attitude wouldn't undermine the positive growth that was taking place in their daughter.

"Our first mistake was to give her everything she wanted when she was growing up."

"We thought, if we could afford it," Mr. Lambert interjected, "why withhold it from her?"

Chelsea nodded solemnly. "I was spoiled rotten." Then, to clarify, she added, "Of course, that doesn't excuse what I did."

Mrs. Lambert continued. "And as she grew older, we may have given her a little too much freedom, a little too soon. And, well, now she's a young mother." Her voice broke over an emotion she'd been apparently been holding in check for some time.

"What's done is done," Mary said. "It does no one any good now to beat yourselves up over what you may or may not have done differently in the past."

Mr. Lambert seemed to concur. "We just wanted you to understand where we were coming from."

"We"—Mrs. Lambert shot another glance at her husband—"I mean, *I* was embarrassed at first by Chelsea's unplanned pregnancy. And I didn't want our very conservative friends and business associates to know how badly we had messed up as parents. So we sent Chelsea to live with her grandmother until we could figure out how to break the news to them."

"Worse things than adding a sweet little baby to the world have happened to families," Mary said. Besides, teen pregnancies were so common these days that they had lost a lot of the stigma that used to surround unwed expectant mothers. It sounded as though Chelsea's parents were worried that the situation could have cost them some business deals, or perhaps their standing in certain social circles.

"We were just getting used to the idea of becoming grandparents," the new grandfather continued, "when we learned about the credit card trouble."

Mrs. Lambert placed her hand on her husband's knee. "He was furious."

He then placed his hand on top of hers. "I got over it, and Susannah and I arranged to pay for all the items that couldn't be returned or sold on eBay."

Mary stirred her tea and wondered how this was any different than giving their daughter everything she had wanted as a child.

Darius who had remained silent until now, finally spoke up. "Chelsea and I talked about it, and we're going to pay her parents back a little every month until the balance is paid off. After her volunteering at the clinic is done, she'll get a job, and all that money will go toward the debt. We're going to do this," he said, and squeezed his wife's shoulder, "even if it takes until we're really old. Like, fifty."

Now it was Mary's turn to cringe.

Having had enough of being still, the baby whimpered and fidgeted. The pink receiving blanket bobbed and danced with the movement of her fists and feet.

"May I hold her?" Mary asked.

With the baby in her arms, it all came back in a flash. As with riding a bicycle, you never lose the knack. Mary swayed from side to side and jiggled the pacifier in the baby's mouth to try to ease her fussiness.

The baby's grandmother leaned forward and smiled at the little darling as if she couldn't get enough of looking at her. "Mary, we also want to thank you for your role in mentoring Chelsea and for sharing your words of wisdom. It sounds as though your talk of personal integrity was what prompted her to insist on paying off the debt herself."

"It truly was a pleasure spending time with the girls," she admitted. There had been times when she'd felt guilty for getting as much or more out of the book club discussions as she had put into them.

Adding to what his wife had said, Mr. Lambert sheepishly acknowledged, "We may have inadvertently taught our daughter that money can buy love and acceptance."

Mrs. Lambert agreed. "But we're not going to make that mistake again. This time, we're going to spoil our granddaughter with love, not stuff." To emphasize her point, she smiled down at the baby and tickled her toe.

Mary gazed down at the precious child who squirmed in her arms. What a blessing from God. With the proper upbringing and guidance from her parents and extended family, Mary prayed the child would grow up to become a fine young woman, as her mother was now turning out to be.

"Her name is Adele," Chelsea said. "It means noble."

Mary smiled, first at Chelsea, then at the little bundle of loveliness. She liked to think that *noble* was exactly the kind of person her young friend would raise this child to become.

ABOUT THE AUTHOR

In addition to her mystery writing, Carolyn Greene is a best-selling romance author. She has been nominated twice for the RITA Award, once for the HOLT Medallion Award, and was presented the Romantic Times WISH Award. Like the main character in this book, Carolyn loves books and welcomes the chance to share her faith through her occupational calling. She and her husband have two children and live in Virginia with their two hyperactive miniature pinschers.

A CONVERSATION WITH CAROLYN GREENE

———◆◆◆———

Q: *Mary volunteers at the "pay as you may" health clinic. In what ways do you give back to your community?*

A: Funny you should ask. As I mentioned in the Dear Reader letter at the front of the book, my daughter's first child is due to make her arrival soon, so I'm looking forward to some babysitting in my future. That said, I'm the last person you'd want to call on to help in the church nursery. For some reason, I feel so helpless when it comes to calming a little one whose personality (and persistent cries!) I don't know.

So I prefer to give back in other ways. Perhaps by mentoring a young writer or leading a Bible study group. After losing fifteen pounds last year by adopting a whole-food, plant-based diet, I'm currently looking into starting a support group for ladies in my community who want to honor the bodies God gave them by eating healthy, unprocessed food as Daniel did in the Bible.

Q: *What inspired you to write a book dealing in part with teen pregnancy?*

A: Honestly? My editors. Some people think of editors as red-pen-bearing fanatics who love to slash and burn words that are so carefully crafted by writers. Not true. I've found the Guideposts editorial team to be creative and caring, with hearts aligned toward addressing the issues that readers face in their everyday lives, all while giving them well-written stories they can identify with and enjoy.

So when my editors suggested we have Mary mentor some pregnant teens, I happily embraced the idea. And I was especially glad that they approved my approach of compassion over condemnation.

Q: *You dedicated this book to your two grown children. Do you have any interesting pregnancy tales of your own to share?*

A: Stephanie was my first. Before she was born, her hands and feet fluttered like a little ballerina. (She eventually went on to take dance classes for more than a dozen years.) Accompanying those prenatal movements were strange popping sounds. It wasn't until after her birth that I discovered the noises, similar to the cracking of a knuckle, were coming from her shoulder. Fortunately, her muscles quickly strengthened from crawling, and the popping eventually stopped.

Chad came three years later. Unlike his sister, he kicked like a goal-scoring soccer player. Despite his vigorous activity, our cat liked to climb up on us, straddle my huge belly, wrap her front legs around my neck, and sleep with her head on my shoulder. It didn't matter to her that her perch jumped around like a basketful of kittens. Now, so many years later, Chad is still a high-energy guy and has even ridden his bicycle across America, from ocean to ocean.

Q: *What traits do you and Mary have in common?*

A: Curiosity would be one. And solving puzzles is another. What we don't have in common is her ability to get her job done at the bookshop no matter how many other things are going on in her life. Somehow, she always manages to solve mysteries, maintain personal relationships, and get the important things done. (Perhaps I should hire an assistant who's as efficient as Mary's bookshop employee, Rebecca!) Even so, as someone with attention deficit disorder (ADD), I admire Mary's ability to focus no matter what else is going on around her. And, as someone who values God, family, and friendships, I especially admire her ability to prioritize and her knack for balancing God, work, and the people in her life.

Q: *Mary loves concocting homemade ice-cream recipes. Have you ever made ice cream? What's your favorite flavor?*

A: No, I haven't made ice cream and rarely eat it. In recent years, I've discovered I feel better when I avoid dairy. However, there is a healthy treat I like just as much, using my favorite flavor combination: peanut butter and chocolate!

In a powerful blender, blend two fresh or frozen ripe bananas, 1 rounded tablespoon cocoa powder, 1 rounded tablespoon peanut butter, two tablespoons chia seeds, about three or four cups of crushed ice, and enough almond milk to give it a thick milkshake consistency. For a sweeter milkshake, drizzle in a tablespoon of honey. To add a healthy protein and increase creaminess, blend in two heaping tablespoons of white beans. (You can't taste the beans ... I promise.) Makes about five or six cups of frosty goodness.

Q: *Some of Mary's grandchildren live far away from her. Do you think it's possible for grandparents and grandchildren to have a close, loving relationship despite many miles separating them?*

A: Oh, wow, stick the knife in and turn it, why don't you? Now you have me missing my granddaughter before she's even born.

Although I don't have experience with grandchildren yet, I have been fortunate to keep a close relationship with my daughter and son, despite their living six hundred and 1,400 miles away, respectively.

People often lament the lack of connection that comes with increasing levels of technology, but I've found that e-mails, texts, Skype, FaceTime, Facebook, and unlimited long-distance calls are essential for keeping up with my loved ones and their day-to-day lives. In addition, we are blessed to live in a time of safe, convenient travel, which means plenty of opportunities for in-person hugs. And, with my laptop computer at the ready, I can write whether at home or traveling to visit my loved ones.

Q: *What's your favorite type of book to read?*

A: I have two favorites: mysteries and romance novels. Although, when you really think about it, romance can be as puzzling and confusing as any mystery, as happens with Mary in *Words of Wisdom*. Most of all, I enjoy stories that help to make sense of the difficult things that happen in people's lives and which lead to a helpful learning experience.

In addition, I'll soon be dusting off some old favorites to read to, or share with, the little one: *Good Dog Carl* by Alexandra Day, *Are You My Mother?* by P. D. Eastman, Phyllis Whitney's *Secret of the Emerald Star*, Walter Farley's *Black Stallion* series... and all those wonderful Bible stories, of course.

HONEY ICE CREAM

3 cups milk
3 cups cream
7 tablespoons sugar
2 vanilla beans, split lengthwise and scraped to loosen up
the small seeds inside the vanilla pod
10 egg yolks
½ cup honey

Bring milk, cream, sugar, and vanilla beans (and the scraped seeds) to a boil. Remove from heat and let infuse for an hour. Whisk together egg yolks and honey until thick and ribbonlike.

In a saucepan, bring the cream and milk mixture back to a boil. While whisking constantly, pour half of the cream and milk mixture into the yolk and honey mixture. Pour this mixture back into the saucepan with the remaining cream and milk mixture.

Over medium heat, cook the sauce while stirring constantly. Cook until the sauce thickens and reaches 185 degrees.

Immediately pour through a fine strainer. Chill the ice-cream mixture in ice water until completely cold. When the mixture is cold, pour into an ice-cream machine and churn until frozen to a soft ice-cream consistency.

Remove from the ice-cream maker and place in a previously frozen container. Cover well and store in a freezer until needed.

FROM THE GUIDEPOSTS ARCHIVES

---◆◆◆---

O my God, I trust in thee: let me not be ashamed....
—Psalm 25:2

I received an e-mail update from a friend of mine living in Boston. It has not been a good year for her. Her father died from cancer, she broke up with her boyfriend and now she has found out she's pregnant.

This is ironic, because she is deeply religious. But she didn't use the word *ironic*; she used the word *shame*.

During the difficult visit to the obstetrician, she had many questions, but she couldn't stop crying long enough to ask them. Finally she confessed that she had always viewed pregnant single girls as either "incredibly stupid or incredibly selfish."

The obstetrician was quiet for a moment, then said, "Or they're incredibly human."

It was exactly the right thing to say—for her, for me and now for you. My friend is carrying a child; you and I are carrying all sorts of things, too, but our baggage is less obvious. Some of what we carry is stupid and selfish, but what she carries is incredibly human. You would think we'd see the irony of that, but we do not. We march on doggedly, blind to our own faults and only too eager to shame others for their sins.

Maybe my friend should name her child after the obstetrician, but I've already thought of other names. I think the baby should be called Wonderful. Or Counselor.

Sorry, I'm getting my stories of young girls in difficult circumstances mixed up.

Lord, no matter how faithful I may think I am, I'm human too. Keep my friend and her baby and all of us close to You.

—Mark Collins

A NOTE FROM THE EDITORS

We hope you enjoy Secrets of Mary's Bookshop, created by the Books and Inspirational Media Division of Guideposts, a nonprofit organization. In all of our books, magazines and outreach efforts, we aim to deliver inspiration and encouragement, help you grow in your faith, and celebrate God's love in every aspect of your daily life.

Thank you for making a difference with your purchase of this book, which helps fund our many outreach programs to the military, prisons, hospitals, nursing homes and schools. To learn more, visit GuidepostsFoundation.org.

We also maintain many useful and uplifting online resources. Visit Guideposts.org to read true stories of hope and inspiration, access OurPrayer network, sign up for free newsletters, download free e-books, join our Facebook community, and follow our stimulating blogs.

To learn about other Guideposts publications, including the best-selling devotional *Daily Guideposts*, go to ShopGuideposts.org, call (800) 932-2145 or write to Guideposts, PO Box 5815, Harlan, Iowa 51593.

Sign up for the

Guideposts Fiction Newsletter

and stay up-to-date on the Guideposts fiction you love!

You'll get sneak peeks of new releases, hear from authors of your favorite books, and even receive special offers just for you.

And it's free!

Just go to

Guideposts.org/newsletters

today to sign up.